Bedside Manner

David J Winters

{Subgenre:Publishers}

Contents

Also by David J. Winters

Interventionism

Roger Jech doesn't have any superpowers, but he has a super ability: harm him, harm yourself in equal measure. Hit him with a right hook, your jaw breaks. Shoot him in the head, your brains blow out the back of you. Drop him in a war zone, your enemies kill themselves killing him. Jech's a weapon to the wrong people and a savior to the right, but before he can become the former, he must learn to harness his gift before it becomes his curse.

THE TAKING OF SHALE CITY

Shale City has seen better days. First, the dam burst, flooding out the town's iron mine. Then, local officials shut down the shipping and courier services, the only thing keeping Shale City hanging on... It was all the mayor of Shale could do to fight off the more 'legitimate' of sleazeballs trying to destroy her city, but now it seems as though some other kind of sleazeball force is encroaching upon her town, set on putting the final nail in its coffin...

SCARCITY

Twenty-one to forty-five-year-old armed forces members, police officers, and intelligence agents (our intended protectors) are going missing everywhere. Seemingly 'taken' out of strange agrarian communes popping up all over the planet. Now Agent Bart, fresh out of retirement, is determined to solve the mystery of these disappearances and get his people back.

ISBN 9780991680368 (paperback) | ISBN 9780991680375 (hardcover) | ISBN 9780991680351 (electronic book)

Cover Font is 'Dirty Seven'. License Number 4697. Licensor: *Flawless and Co.*

{SubGenre : Publishers}
www.subgenrepublishers.com

For mom, for inspiring the nurse in Eminence Gray
For Clint Eastwood, for inspiring the cop

Chapter 1

Means of Production

The four sit in conversation. They sit in those wide, high-backed plush chairs that make a person look like a fingernail of a fingertip of a velveteen Kong. They can't be all that comfortable though, not in those suits. Might also be the stage they're on, their fingertippy perches arced in a bone-breaking semicircle to face a crowd of hundreds where, of our conversationalists, no more than two are wired for the grandstanding the night requires. There isn't a single value shared between the four either. At least the four as depicted. This is a debate you see, framed as a conversation between the representatives of a grade-schooler's binary, but one thus far consisting of filibuster.

The event crowd sits in much less comfortable chairs, demonstrably so, vinyl-thicker-than-cushion uncomfortable. They're packed into that twenty-five hundred-seat amphitheater too. Knees fused to knees. Elbows fused to elbows. Crowd may still win the night's comfort game however as the aesthetic pleasures born of an enlighten-ment, hopefully to come, serve as analgesic. Individuals of all walks of life, identities, and socio-economic backgrounds constitute the crowd, where the only tie binding them outside of human universals is an interest in the subject at hand.

Despite the unwavering interests of the audience, a large LED array beams the night's theme at them from the back of the stage. It beams in an ironical manner, evidently, featuring an animated Amerikan flag with the following written across it, waving in rhythm to the flag,

Unionization and The Market.

Of the four on the stage, Nina Burgess speaks. She's directing her attention to event moderator Diane Saint. Periodically, between the default image of the LED flag waving, a low-framerate video of the speakers plays for audience members in the back. Naturally, Burgess is featured. The chyron under her stilted LED representation reads,

Janine Burgess
President of the United Parcel Workers Union (UPWU)

"It's true you see," Burgess insists to the moderator. "It really is. It's no platitude. The worker *is* the lifeblood of industry. Of society. But the worker has had their spirit of solidarity stripped from them by certain... *machinations* you might say... of the West. This so-called virtue of individualism that has convinced folks to only ever 'go it alone'. As though the greatest impropriety in the world is cooperation. It's denied the workers their greatest tool: collective action." Burgess turns to the audience. "But, like a single wayward blood cell cannot nourish our vital organs, a single worker cannot ensure society the resources it needs to survive.

What's good for the blood is good for the body as a whole. The brain of the body understands this. It doesn't starve our cells of oxygen just because they function collectively." Burgess pauses a second, leans closer to the audience like she's sharing an aside just for them. "*For-profit* executives on the other hand..."

A few in the crowd chuckle.

"Blood also clots," says Charlie Reime not as hushed as intended. He's caught Saint's attention as well as the guy manning the array.

Charles Reime
CEO of Park-Mart Department Stores

"What was that Mr. Reime?"

He waves away any further attention.

Saint returns to Burgess. "And so, what's your secret Ms. Burgess? In just eighteen months the *yoo-pee-triple-yoo* has collectivized the entire of the warehouse and courier services workforce for both *Alom* and *EchoNet*, the two largest online distributors in the country. How'd you do it?"

Burgess is contemplative a second, then... "I don't want to sound fatalistic, but I think the reason for the success of these unions has to do with the fact that... *It's time.* Late-stage capitalists, with their regimentation and their hierarchies of control, have managed to delay the return of the social instinct in us, an instinct for the good of all of us, but these functionaries still constitute a *late* stage, a finite stage therefore, a stage that has to come to an end. If I deserve credit for anything, it's for merely maintaining morale. Merely handing the worker a life-preserver with which to keep their head above the waves of history."

There's some scattered applause.

3

. . .

THE CORPSE OF THE YOUNG man lies in the park.

They call it a park but it's really just a tenth of an acre of sod and a single tree plopped down between the monoliths of affordable housing. The intent was to make the space a little less depressing, maybe give the kids a place to play. Or, maybe they wanted to add a more bucolic feel to a shortcut used exclusively by criminals of whom stray bullets either originate or terminate? Because that's about all they achieved. Might not be a complete waste though. You can't say there isn't a world of off-the-books entrepreneurs taking their shoes off to enjoy a stroll through the Blue Bermuda when the cops aren't around. Can't say it now however because those cops *are* around.

Detective *Eminence Gray* works next to her partner and newbie detective *Jon Bomn*. Em's putting on a latex glove from a rudimentary forensics satchel: cops call it a *rude bag*. It hangs off a get-up that isn't stylish but well-put-together and serviceable: a simple pantsuit. Bomn forgot his rude bag so there's nothing to hang from his modern suit that's a too-blue shade of blue atop those tan dress shoes all the twenty-five to forty-five-year-old kids are wearing. He looks preppy. Looks like Justin Trudeau. But don't worry, his naïveté is wearing away fast.

The detectives hunker over the corpse of the man, mid-twenties. The dead man wears jeans and a car coat over a hoodie. Em puts her latex-gloved hand on the dead man's midsection, patting it down.

Detective Sergeant *Richard 'Dickie' Tesque*—crumpled charcoal suit—gets to the scene. He half observes, half participates, half philosophizes. *Half, half, and half.* That's the math. The math and unofficial motto of West Brandon Robbery/Homicide.

Here're the theories.

"Terf kill. Up and comers making a point," Tesque asserts approaching the two investigators.

"Robbery," Em corrects.

"He's got a pocket full of patches and his wallet, cash still inside. I'm up to speed?"

Em shakes her head at the superior. "He's a runner. He's out here, he's got a bag of product the size of your head or a few thousand in cash. Always one of the two, never both. Tonight's neither."

"Well, if that's the dilemma, you've got your anomaly. You sure?"

She pulls open the kid's hoodie. We see he's got a fanny pack on his hip, front compartment wide open. "See this?"

"Wore one in '91. Mine was fluorescent as hell though. Fuckin' rad."

Em looks with rebuke at Tesque's flippancy. He doesn't mean anything by it. He's just trying to turn it off. Not appropriate in front of the newbie though.

Sarge looks begrudging, speaks at Bomn. "Compartmentalizing newb. Learn it."

Em gets back to the case. "These things were making a comeback among twenty-fives to forty-fives. Back out of fashion now. The Rock hasn't worn his in years." She flips the pack forward a little. "This one comes with a money belt. Empty."

She takes out some side cutters from her rude bag. She flips up the seam hiding the zipper to the compartment, clips a little padlock on the zipper tab with the side cutters and unzips. The compartment is empty of cash just as Em prognosticated.

Bomn marvels a little. "How?"

Em looks at Tesque. *Would you like to field this one Sergeant?*

"Your derivation detective," Tesque insists.

"Dilemma," she recommences. "He took the drugs or cash. He gets the cash, no drugs, so he'd hafta bring the fentanyl patches to plant."

Bomn looks like he's doing a grade-school word problem in his head.

CLACK!

Em snaps a finger at a wandering Bomn. *Keep up rook.*

"No way a user this desperate gets his hands on a dozen patches *before* a robbery. A wallet with twenty-two bucks in it, not so tough. He got to the drugs not the cash. Woulda missed the cash anyways." Em tosses the broken padlock to Bomn. "Thief pops the kid a couple times in the chest with something low caliber, grabs all but a couple dozen of the patches, leaves them and the wallet. Gone." She takes a foldable card caddy out of the hidden compartment on the fanny pack, looks to Tesque, "Round up the usuals. Eighty/twenty we find the killer dead from the patches or whoever killed him to get to them. I don't want this shit to go on and on. If we're quick, we might get lucky and stumble onto the happiest pre-mortem poo-butt in the world."

"Pre-mortem?" Bomn asks, confused.

"Christ newbie! You take the detective's exam or get a learner's permit?" Tesque refocuses on the officer of seniority. "Em, your chain of inference, it's tight but not fact."

"The victim was robbed and robbed for the drugs." She waves the wallet. "This was a plant and a shit one. He's not robbing to sell. Patches out there are as good as marked bills. He'd be painting a target on his back if he tried. He took 'em anyway. Personal consumption. He was hoping for powder. Something booted. This is his consolation prize." Em can see Tesque isn't moving on it. She changes tack. "I'll take any fall with the higher-ups."

Sergeant's off the hook. He's lovin' Em's theory now. "Ballsy. I can't have the major taking my head off this week. You follow up on this and I'll flex sack next time."

"*Right* Dickie."

Tesque gestures to the card caddy Em's holding. She gets it. She gives a hint of an *again?* grimace. Tesque gives a less hinty *your turn* shrug. She relents.

"Newbie and I'll notify next of kin."

SAINT NODS APPRECIATIVELY AT BURGESS just finishing her point. It's customary. Saint turns to *management* so to speak. "Mr. Reime, Mr. Park, you're both outspoken critics of unionization. Do you feel—"

"*Capitalist pigs!*" shouts a protestor from the back.

Saint adjusts accordingly. "Sorry about that. Do you feel your time is coming to an end?"

Neither of the men are expected to speak first but it's Reime who does. "Absolutely not," he protests. "If Ms. Burgess is so certain a 'spirit of solidarity' has overtaken the workers she represents, ask her why support for unionization only grew *after* suppression of our secret-ballot voting laws—laws she lobbied so hard to eliminate. Why's she so afraid to let the workers speak their minds anonymously, free of fear of coercion and reprisal?" Reime leans backward and cocks his head in order to talk directly to Saint, occluding Burgess from the conversation in the process. "You see Ms. Saint, Marxist dialectics notwithstanding... Because they don't... Our employees, prior to the *de facto* repeal of those ballot laws, repeatedly and consistently voted against unions." He leans forward to let Burgess see him again. "How's that for solidarity?" He returns to the occlusion. "When given the opportunity to voice their opinions free of repercussions, we see that the workers time and time again are against the notion. We at Park-Mart aren't opposed to unions Ms. Saint, the people under our employ are, and we respect that."

A small section of the crowd erupts in boos and jeers. A lot of derisive sloganeering too. They chant things like, "Pock-Mark pigs!" over and over and hold signs that read,

Pock-Mark has got to go!
Exploiters! Propagators of oppressive power structures!
Pock-Mark is a rash on society!
Etc.

Saint looks to the small group of very vocal, surprisingly closer to middle-aged than youthful, protestors. "Please, there will be plenty of time for the voicing of concerns during the Q&A to follow. Please..."

Amidst the protestors' clamor, a man in his fifties wearing a shirt with *CONWU* on it—not *yoo-pee-triple-yoo* but he's definitely a union man—stands. He's large, imposing. The kind of imposing you know isn't even dialed up to five on a scale of fifty yet. He turns to the protestors and starts eating them up with his eyes. A few more audience members stand to back him up as the protestors back down. They don't *sit* down, though they're hushed. Saint sees the significance of this and gestures for one of the nearby event organizers to give the man a microphone. The room goes real silent for a place with twenty-five hundred people in it.

The man is at first surprised by the mic issued at him, then reluctant. However, seeing as all eyes are on him, he accepts that he's obliged to say *something* to the protestors.

He takes the mic in hand and speaks calmly and coolly like he's all our dads. "You all." He waves a wave that encompasses the protestors and no one else. "You all are here from the suburbs and the ivory towers everywhere because you enjoy play acting like you want to tear it all down. Everyone else is here because we're trying to figure out how to make a living—some *just* a living, some *at least* a living—but we all want to make that living in the system you all just take for granted. Please, sit down."

The crowd applauds. Some cheer.

The protestors are definitely not interested in civility but the thinning patience of attendees, present to hear good faith dialecticians and not the censoriate, is palpable. The activists cower for the time being.

Saint gets everyone back on track. "Well, I think the people have spoken and what they've said is *we want this conversation to continue.* Ms. Burgess, it also looks like our outspoken member of the Construction Workers Union of Amerika could give you a run for your money, should he ever get into parcel shipping."

Burgess smiles at Saint. "Diane, the song of solidarity comes from a chorus of millions. My voice is but one of many."

"And *that* provides a perfect segue back to the topic at hand," Saint acknowledges. "What say you Ms. Burgess? It *is* true that when given a voice, the average Amerikan worker expresses no desire to unionize..."

Burgess doesn't miss a beat. "Only because, as I said— and I'm sure our *CONWU* brother will attest to this— Western society has taught us that anything other than rugged individualism is blasphemy." Burgess leans forward in her chair in order to talk across Saint and directly to Reime for rebuttal. "It's merely a coincidence the *Worker*

Liberation Act passed at the same time working folks realized there's room for them atop management's precious hierarchy. Contrary to what they've been conditioned to believe their whole lives, working folks have finally come to understand that they can—and *should*—lean on each other."

Reime leans forward Mirroring Burgess. "If the people are so lacking in agency and, so, are susceptible to the kinds of indoctrination you speak of—via god knows what societal mechanisms—then the last thing they need is another opportunist telling them how to work and how to earn."

"You're the only one exploiting working folks Mr. Reime," Burgess fires.

"Am I? You'll never guarantee the wages we pay our workers." Reime affects an ingratiating tone at the crowd. "You see, at Park-Mart we've always paid well above minimum wage. We pay higher because we don't buy inferior products. The worker has a product to sell: her labor. And we in management, the customers essentially, want the best quality product and that costs a premium. If we can't buy your superior product at this premium because collective agreements force us to keep ineffective laborers under our employ, then you, the effective laborer, will have to settle for some minimum wage job elsewhere. Or no job at all... Companies simply cannot afford to pay you what you're worth when they're subsidizing workers who are not a good fit. A position filled by the wrong person for the job means one less position for you. A position filled by the wrong person for the job means less revenue for the organization. This means less pay to go around, hence lower wages for all." He turns back to Burgess. "This is what unionization gets you. Just look at Alom and EchoNet's plummeting share prices..."

"Shares you've been selling off by the ton."

"Nothing illegal about using publicly available information to predict market trends."

"But is it moral? Betting on a business to fail?"

"Why don't you ask your soon-to-be *former* members that when these investments are paying them double-minimum-wage at Park..."

EM DRIVES, BOMN RIDES. THE radio crackles the following:

> *...with yoo-pee-triple-yoo workers in strike position, a final 'no' vote this Monday will mean the largest labor strike in Amerikan history...*

Em's taking her pulse, looking at her FatButt™ fitness tracker, steering with her knees. Those pant suit pants are a little slick. Her car weaves in and out of its lane when the fabric slips off the wheel. She pops a sublingual melatonin under her tongue. Her fingers are back on her pulse.

> *...BUMPUMP BUMPUMP BU... THUMP! BUMPUMP BUMPUMP BU... THUMP!...*

Bomn, who's usually hyper-aware of Em's inopportune stress management, is distant. He starts speaking and it's all rote.

"Detective, department regulations dictate I apologize on behalf of the sergeant."

Em frowns a frown that started all the way back at *regulations*. "For what?"

"For that remark about your balls."

"My *balls*?"

Bomn flusters. He doesn't want to be having this

conversation. Nobody does. "N—Not *your* balls... The balls he said you had. The *ballsy flexing sack* thing."

"You denyin' me my balls Bomn?"

More fluster. Department regulations aren't what they used to be. "D—Do you have... Do you want *ball*... Do you ident—"

"Christ Newbie! You went to that *Workplace Equity and Safety* seminar didn't you! You sound like one of my daughter's term papers. Got a good head but my god! If she's not careful her ed degree's gonna send her around the bend. Everything's a social construction but her tuition bill. What do you notice about dummies who take stupid risks?"

Newb's aback at his partner's discursiveness. He scrambles for a response. "Risks?"

"Yeah, the people we book who take swings at TAC guys. We catch swimming upstream after they jump off a bridge to evade arrest. Who eat bullets. *Literally!* Remember that guy in West Brandon East who thought any gun was legal as long as it didn't have ammo? Ate the whole clip's worth!" Em puts on her best Clint Eastwood, "*I can't remember if I shit six bullets, or only five...* Had to serve a search warrant and a Fleet Enema!"

Em laughs. Bomn tries to follow.

"What'a'ya notice?" she demands.

"Uh..."

"Come on! Give a suspect description that would fit any one of the above."

Bomn hesitates. Looks at Em with narrow in his eyes for a second. She churns her hand at him. Then... "Uh, alright. *Suspect... Male—*"

"That's right Bomn! They're dudes!" She revels a little. "You look at the subset of humanity that takes the most extreme of risks, from the bravest of heroes to the most impetuous of idiots, the vast majority are men. You know why?"

"Because society—"

"*Society* nothing! It's testosterone Bomn. And where does testosterone come from?"

Newbie hesitates again, like he knows the answer but *regulation dictates...*

"Come on Newb, it's not a test. Not a test to tickle my fancy. *Test to tickle...* Shit Bomn. Testicles. Testosterone comes from testicles. Yer brave, ya take risks. Ya take risks, ya got testosterone. Ya got testosterone, ya got balls. Yer ballsy!"

She starts taking her pulse again. Bomn puts both hands on the dash.

"It's a compliment Bohm. The only thing Dickie's guilty of is being a crass fuckin' bastard when it comes to his compliments. Unlike us sophisticates..." She opens her window and spills the last of her coffee out the cup. "You know, once, just once, I'd like those seminar prudes to get a taste of the job before heading back to wherever it is the middle-upper class go when they're not telling the working class how to think. Ninety-nine percent of the time we turn over a kid face down in the dirt, like tonight, we gotta wash the *XY* chromosomes off our hands and they wanna cry phallocentrism for talk of ballsacks?" Fingers go back to neck. Knees back to wheel.

There's a silence a few seconds.

How should you respond to all this rook? How's about: as we all would under such circumstances. As we do behind closed doors realizing yet another workaday everyman or everywoman finds establishmentarian orthodoxies as stupid as those orthodoxies are. Bomn's relieved at his mentor's iconoclasm. Mentor notices.

"What's my rep around here Bomn?"

"*Rep?*"

"What's my nickname around here? I know you know 'em. You can say 'em."

"Th—they call you *Florence Nightingale*. Sometimes. But mostly *Empathy Gray*. Both on account of you used to be a nurse."

"Empathy Gray. *Empathy* Bomn. Empathy isn't caring yet they say I have that quality too don't they?"

"Yeah."

"Bet you're not thinkin' that after your first week on the job with me are ya Bomn?"

"Yeah," he repeats, this time a little wry.

"Yet caring ain't compassion, but they say I've got that too don't they?"

"Yup."

"Those masculine qualities Bomn?" Em's saying *Bomn* like a bell gonging at this point.

"Nope."

"They resent me for those qualities Bomn?"

"Nah."

"They think me a man when I use 'em to make an arrest Bomn?"

"No."

"Care to reassess the logic of those seminar prudes in light of the facts Bomn?"

Hushed, "You're right."

"What?"

Louder, "You're right."

Em softens on the kid, gives him a second to process things before her recapitulation. Then... "Listen, don't take my busting your... *chops* personally. You can be a sentimentalist on this job. You can be a rationalist. You should be both. The one thing you can't afford to not be is a realist. You don't want to be a realist on this job you can go join my daughter in one of her curriculum implementation courses. You got it?"

"Yeah."

Em can't resist...

"Do you want ball?"

Bomn laughs. Em joins him.

THE OLD MAN LETS OUT a wearied sigh. He appears ambiguously, possibly generally upset by the evening's proceedings. Diane Saint notices.

"Mr. Park, we've yet to hear from you tonight. What do you think of all this?"

Old...

"I'm sorry, what was that Mr. Park?" she asks.

"Oh, Ms. Saint... I'm old." He says this meditative, eyes closed. "My weathered mind can't keep up with the pace of the politics apparent in all things business these days." Eyes open. "I'm old fashioned too. You have to remember, I was there when our first *Park Market* opened, my parents and my four siblings living in a one-bedroom apartment above it, running everything. I'm old... Old fashioned... Though I'll try my best to keep pace."

Bertrand Park
Majority shareholder and son of the founder of Park-Mart
Department Stores.

He appears to be sizing his interlocutors up, deciding whose point to address first. He looks to Burgess and settles. "Ms. Burgess," he begins. "We're not a charity. If an employee generates more revenue we pay him more. If he generates less we pay him less. We pay our employees a function of what they generate for the organization and if they fall below a certain earnings threshold, we end their employment. If we didn't, efficiency would drop to unsustainable levels and this would end *everybody's* employment. This happens all the time with your unionized workers. There's not a collective agreement in the world that says employees must be paid with money the company doesn't earn." He grins a little. "Getting blood from a stone is something even union executives haven't figured out yet..."

The crowd laughs. Even the union guys liked that one. Burgess nods in concession.

"Can't get blood from a stone," Park reiterates. "Can't get profit from inefficiency. It's the way of the market." He's been quite gracious with Burgess but now his look turns stern. That look turns to Reime. "All this said, my dear boy Charlie, your model is not correct either."

Reime smiles at this, uneasy look to it. "W—Well, let no one ever suggest me the exception to the rule *there's always wisdom to be gained from Bertie Park.*"

Park is deadpan at this. "Those of us executives aren't customers of any sort buying labor," he says. "We own and maintain—what we'll refer to as that concept you were so fond of discussing in the papers you used to publish Ms. Burgess—a means of production." Burgess smiles politely at this. Park nods. "We conceived of, created, and maintain a means of production. Others who are qualified may use it for their own ends, but for a fee, a cut of what they generate. Like if I had a fishing boat that I built and maintained. I'd lend the boat to you, you'd catch a number of fish, and my fee would be, say, three of your fish for every five. This model allows our workers the security of not having to procure and maintain their own means, and it grants us the freedom to focus on the integrity of ours and not production and distribution. This was always my father's preferred model of worker/employer relationship, and it's always been mine. It's a symbiotic relationship. We need laborers as much as they need us. There's just fewer of *us*, you see."

Burgess is activated by talk of *means of production*. "This relationship entails your having complete control of said means. You admit this?"

"And to having created it and having maintained it on my family's own time and our own dime... And for the last two generations." He uncrosses his legs and leans forward to better see Burgess. He's lightly massaging both knees as he speaks. "These businesses don't just fall out of the sky Ms. Burgess, where my father was the first to stumble upon a Park-Market one day, only to hide it away from the world behind lock and key. These organizations require ingenuity, time, energy, and materials... as well as luck... to generate. This is a lifelong commitment that I can't just walk away from, unlike the worker who may walk away at any time for a better means. Only a tiny handful of people on this earth can maintain this business with the same effectiveness as my family." Reime puts a hand on Park's shoulder in a gesture of support. The gesture goes unrequited, almost conspicuously. "That's the tradeoff. Any one of my employees wants to put in his own time, energy, and funds necessary to maintain our stores, to the same degree of effectiveness as my family, is welcome to. But I wouldn't wish that burden on my worst enemy."

Burgess remains exercised. "You'll pardon me if I can't sympathize with someone who demands his employees generate far more than they need to sustain themselves, just to maintain a surplus for him. After all, you're not sending fisherpersons out in your boat, so to speak, just to catch the two fish a day they need to feed their families."

"True, there are always quotas as well as time constraints. And, when you have as many workers as we do at Park, it becomes an averages game. Average rate of production over time. Our workers do generate more output than they require personally, but don't forget, *so to speak*, it's roughly two out of every three fish put back into overhead and operation costs."

"One from five is still more than you and your executives will ever need."

"*Necessity* being the least cut and dried of all philosophical concepts, I'm sure you'll agree Ms. Burgess. Although the metaphor long past tired, if it weren't for our 'boats', worker and owner alike would be bent over waist-deep in the drink praying for some slippery cod to swim right into his arms. Some may have more than others in this world but it's the idea that all have *at least* what they need that should be of greatest concern. Our workers have and they wouldn't if it weren't for people like my father. And you seem to be forgetting Ms. Burgess, you can always go off and build your own boat."

"Not folks in vulnerable gr—"

"*END FREE MARKET TYRANNIES!*"

SPLOOSH!

A cup full of a white chalky liquid smashes up against the shoulder of Park, dousing him. Reime rises to intercept the thrower, now charging at the old man, almost within arm's length. Assailant is swinging some sort of object in a sock at Park as Reime intervenes. Reime bears the brunt of the attack and goes down grabbing his right cheek. Assailant catches sight of security approaching and moves back into the crowd and across the theater aisle. There's a substantial amount of blood pooling under Reime's injury.

Mr. Park calmly wipes the substance off himself watching his middle-aged attacker running off, disappearing through a proscenium exit. He turns to help his CEO.

We leave the chaos with Burgess and Saint hovering over Reime and Park as more security pours in.

Chapter 2

I Know How You Feel

The address on the victim turns out to belong to a family house, a bungalow incidentally. The detectives approach cautiously. Em pays special attention to a woman sitting on the porch of the home. Woman appears to be in her mid-forties. She's chatting with two teenage boys sitting to either side of her. Em continues moving forward, keeping eye contact, wearing a neutral expression. Bomn follows a foot behind, pensive.

Em's about halfway up the walk when she says, "Hello." The woman just looks at her mirroring the neutral expression. Em follows up, "Might Dennis Idris live here?"

The woman's hesitant, a suspicion betrayed in her manner. "This is the Hrominchuk residence," she offers.

"So he doesn't live here? Might you know Dennis?"

Silence from all on the porch, then...

"I ask my daughter if she know anything." The woman gets up to enter her home. She pauses at the door. "Why is it you look?"

"We're just checking an address we found among

Dennis' personal effects," Bomn says. "It's very important we talk to his—"

The woman's posture falters. The older of the two boys looks hit by a ton of bricks while the younger just looks confused, imploring the older for an explanation of what those words imply. Words like *among his personal effects*. The explanation doesn't come.

"Don't say another word," Em growls at Bomn, trying to remain as hushed and discreet as possible.

The woman has slid down to her knees, her face contorting. *"Denni?"* she says in a Ukrainian accent now more pronounced. Grief needs a path of least resistance and maintaining the pretense of a local fluency is resistance by social nicety. She hangs on the screen-door latch, her head shaking in disbelief as her sons move to console her.

Bomn realizes the weight of those words, what he's done. "Sh—she said she didn't know him Em—"

"She said nothing of the sort!" Em speaks in a clipped whisper: *now is not the time.*

A girl, likely the woman's daughter, about fifteen, has come to the screen door. She's confused and scared by the sight. She can't get to her mother on the other side due her mother's collapsed position. This only adds to the girl's torture.

"Ma'am. Ma'am." Em looks back to Bomn, says in a rapid-fire hush, "Think she'd be forthcoming to the people roustin' her son the hundredth time?" She moves briskly and deliberately toward the mother and kids.

The mother cries out in pain.

Bomn's left knee buckles. He reflexively crisscrosses his forearms over his slightly kneeling stronger leg for support. He looks like he's going to vomit. He watches Em to distract himself. He can't hear what she's saying—if she's saying anything—but he can see what she's doing.

She's gotten to the mother still crumpled by the door. Mother's now just mouthing her son's name over and over. Em takes the woman's face in her hands, real gentle, both consoling her and looking deep into her eyes. There's authority in Em, a knowledge betrayed, but also a comforting neutrality. Em gestures for the boys to pull their mother's chair a little closer. As she and the boys lift the woman to the chair, one of Em's arms is wrapped out around the mother's shoulders and the other stretched to mother's wrist, taking her pulse. Em points to the door. Simultaneously, older son runs in as the daughter runs out. Em moves in close to the mother's ear. The mother's in a state of shock, still just repeating her son's name. Em whispers. Whispers more. Then... The mother's face goes still. Color returns to it and emotions creep in. She's crying tears of grief now. Looking into Em's eyes, Mrs. Hrominchuk takes the officer's hand, squeezes. Em squeezes back then moves away as the son and daughter flow in. The three embrace now.

The older son exits the house with a glass of water. He hands it to his mom. Em's observing the mother's condition as—

THUMP!

She turns to see the older son about to smash his fist a second time into a post of the veranda.

THUMP!

Son storms back into the house.

AGAIN, EM DRIVES, BOMN RIDES. Em's determined.

Bomn's contrite—though he appears to be trying to put the contrition on the back burner. Trying to act aloof.

"S—so—" His stutter betrays him. He's not fooling anyone. What he did doesn't make him irredeemable, not by any stretch, but he did cause a family experiencing the most grief they ever will an unnecessary pain in addition. He doesn't want any forgiveness just yet, but he has promised to puke himself empty as soon as he gets home. "Where to now?"

"That kid didn't have grief in his eyes..."

THE OLDER SON HAS PUT on a dark hoodie—hood up and over. He's skulking outside a non-descript house of a residential neighborhood that's experienced better times. It's a typical *defeat or defiance* block. A few of the houses have some combination of boarded-up windows, rotten gray paintless wooden siding, and graffiti tagging all around, while the others are immaculate right down to the wreaths on the doors and the manicured flowerbeds in front. The latter aren't giving in. The defiant have family vehicles in the driveway, the defeated have overpriced luxury SUVs. The son has both hands in the large front pocket of his hoodie.

He climbs up the steps of the house's veranda. Everything's structured, if not maintained, similarly to his own residence so he moves about with ease—stealth-like too. At the second to last step, he pulls his dead brother's .38 revolver out of his hoodie pocket. He slinks along the wall of the front of the house, inching up to the window right of the door. He's about to peek in when he hears a bit of a clamor. He recoils, moves himself into the space between the door and the window. The clamor's followed by an angry voice, muffled by the structure.

"Bottomless pits."

Son listens carefully. Far as he can tell no one's moving any nearer to him. Assured, he creeps back to the window's edge taking that peek. What he sees are three people lying about the living room on various pieces of furniture, passed out, maybe worse. There's a man hovering over them, sober as a monk in a lifeboat. Man's looking down on them in disgust.

"Mother-fuckin' gluttons."

He throws a handful of condom-sized ziplock baggies at the users on the couch.

Son still can't discern if the supine are simply anesthetized or dying or dead. He knows by the shape they're in the middle disjunct's a definite *yes* for much of their life lived to death. If they're alive they're dying and not in the *we're all dying as every second is one closer to death* existentialist sense, but in the sense that their use has taken too many years off. How many they got left? Either way, something gives the kid the impression that *Baggy Man* wouldn't react any differently to these people were they sleeping, slipping, or gone.

"Choke on 'em."

Baggy Man pulls on some Bluetooth headphones and thumps up the stairs, dialing, maybe texting, on his phone.

Son watches the man move around the landing and out of sight. Man's gone, so son carries on. He moves backward toward the door of the house, silent as a dream. He reaches for the knob, gives it a test-of-a-twist. Deadbolt's latched. Of course it is. No choice but to do a one-eighty, head for his bike down the curb.

Has he had a change of heart? Nah. He's there to

retrieve a device, something he has taped to the crossbar of his ten-speed. The device is a goose-neck pry bar. He could have brought it with him at the start if this caper of his, been more economical, but the kid's clearly new to this. He runs an Exacto-style knife across the loops of tape. Device is free. He has it now. He starts back for the house, when...

"I know how you feel..."

Kid stops in his tracks. Spins toward the voice just in time to see Em emerge from the shadows and on into the streetlight's shine.

"...Yer *feelin'* like revenge."

She looks to the house that houses the kid's quarry. "If not for that guy in there your brother wouldn't have been out here and he'd still be alive." She moves closer to him. She crosses an invisible threshold and he flinches backward. She knows to stop a minute. "A boy your brother's age, over in Coughlin, got killed last week delivering pizzas. If not for the sweet old lady who owned the pizzeria, he wouldn't have been out in the streets delivering with a pocket full of cash and he'd still be alive. Is the old lady next on your list?"

Kid doesn't miss a beat. There's flawed logic in this and he's going to exploit it. "Guy in there finds addicts who let him squat for supply. They die from the drugs and he takes the house."

"So what's the math?" Em asks. "You gonna kill him because he's stealing their health and home one dose at a time or are you gonna kill him because the job gets runners killed? Cuz if your math's the former, then I got news for you. You're gonna have to keep killing until you're a convict, a hypocrite, or the perpetrator of the biggest hood holocaust anyone's ever seen cuz guys like that are not going to stop coming." Another step forward. "If your math's the latter, then that sweet old lady's next because apparently employing somebody who dies on the job is a sufficient condition for murdering 'em." Em takes another step forward, stops. "You should be grieving, not killing."

Logic's sound. Kid knows it. "Fuck you."

"You should be with your mom, another sweet old lady, doesn't deserve the punishment. She should be grieving like you should but she's too busy tearing herself to pieces trying to figure out how to keep you safe in this world only nothing's coming to mind because you're out here so she's too busy tearing herself to pieces. That sweet old lady needs real tears that won't come with you stalking these streets." Step. "Go home. Show her your noble soul." Step. "Allow her to grieve your brother." Em's near toe-to-toe. Kid's not backing up anymore. "Please."

The boy's posture starts to falter.

"*Please.*"

He's woozy. His eyes are welling.

"I know how you feel..."

Kid collapses into Em. She holds him up, holding on. She caresses the back of his head.

"Good boy."

EM PARKS. BOMN SITS. ONLY, Bomn's in the backseat. Oldest son sits in the front seat sipping a bottle of water. Traded it for the .38.

Kid's calmed. His eyes are puffy, but he's a stoic. The world needs a stoic and he knows it. Not the kind of stoic where a fool believes he's some sort of essential cog in the machinery of humanity and therefore must set aside emotion to let people walk all over him for some nonexistent greater cause. Not the kind of stoic who believes his being a pushover is necessary for realizing the grand scheme. No, he's a stoic in that he knows his emotions will only get in the way of his shaping... changing... maintaining... that tiny corner of the world he has any control over.

He's no pushover you see. So he sits, calm. Dutiful even.

"I never got your first name," Em says.

"Gregory."

"Not Greg?"

"Gregory," Gregory insists.

"You know who I think of when I hear that name?"

"A person your age? *Gregory Hines.*"

"Ha! You a mind reader?"

"Nah. My mom named me after him."

"Because she liked the idea of a dancer who could play tough guys?"

"Other way around."

Gregory opens the door, *time to leave*. Em follows suit. She moves around the front of her car, carrying on the conversation.

"He played a lot of cops," she says. "Like in that robot movie with the Danish chick?"

"Army colonel, Dutch."

"Thought that was *Predator*..." She issues her card at him. "Either way, he fought crime. If you want to do right in your neighborhood, reach out once in a while."

Gregory takes the card in hand, holds it at arm's length. He's looking at it but he's not reading it. Em notices.

"What? *You ain't no snitch?*"

He looks a little insulted. "*Snitch?* That what they say where you're from? I got no regard for anyone stupid enough to believe there's integrity in keeping his enemy's secrets."

"Not a man of principle?"

"*Principle?* You h'archies* seem to be under the impression our not askin' you for help is a matter of pride." He affects a mocking tone. "*I don't rat! I don't snitch!* They don't ask for help because if they did, whoever's holding their well-being hostage is gonna fuck 'em worse."

"*They?* Not *you?*"

"*Snitchin'*, or whatever you people call it, is just another justified means to a justified end..." He gestures to the general tranquility of his particular block then snaps a picture of Em with an old-timey style film camera from the eighties—*where'd he get that?* "...As any other."

Em's blinking out the afterimage of the flash. "So what's the apprehension?"

"There's a reason you don't see guys my brother ran for in the suburbs. It ain't because they're no pushovers over there. And it sure ain't because they're no riches to steal. And you know it ain't because they don't do drugs."

"Then what?"

Gregory points to the badge hanging out Em's pocket.

"No cops in the suburbs," she says, incredulous.

"No moat in the castle." He opens his water bottle and pours a line between he and Em. "If you can keep them out of there, you can keep them out of here. It's just a matter of your choices. They've always been here."

Logic's sound. Em can't fight him on this one. She reaches to take the card back. He's happy to give it.

"Well, change your mind, call West Brandon switchboard. Ask for *the nurse.*"

Gregory's eyebrow raises a little.

---

* *H'archy* is a common slur in West Brandon. It's pronounced 'har-kee' for *high-hierarchy, high enough on the hierarchy,* etc. Denotes people of sufficient socio-economic means.

The what?

IT'S A ROTE KIND OF night. Once more, Em drives, Bomn rides. Phone rings to break the pattern. Em hits *Answer* on the dash touch screen.

"Any news?" she asks.

"Dead," we hear Tesque say through the car's speakers. "Overdose, like ya said. Patch under the tongue."

"Sign of struggle?"

"Yeah. Guy's a career addict. He's more lesion than skin at this point."

Em grows impatient. "What'a'ya got Dickie?"

Bit of a pause.

"Been a long night Em. Why don't you just drop the rook off and go home to the family?"

"Dick..."

"Alright..."

THE ADDICT'S TIED TO A chair in the alley, eyes bulging out, red, dust having settled on them at this point. There's duct tape around his mouth with a small incision where an evidence tech removed the fentanyl patch. There's also a second unused patch stapled to the addict's forehead. Police and technicians work around the victim.

Tesque's there too, still talking to Em, "...Used a carpenter staple. Real messy."

"Clear a message as any to potential copycats," Em says on the other end. "Think the owner's stupid enough to have taken the rest?"

"Just the two patches here."

"I was just at the guy's front door Dickie."

"Well, then you don't need me to draw you a map. I'll meet you with the relevant paper."

"Exigent circumstances."

"Em?" Silence. "Em..." More silence. "Shit!"

IT'S CALM, QUIET IN FRONT of the dealer's house. It usually is. That's why he picked this location. The conversation between Gregory and Em wasn't going to change that. It was just a conversation after all. Exceptionally quiet and exceptionally calm now though. Maybe it's the calm before...

SCREECH!

Em's car grinds to a halt out front of the house. *Redux.*

Chapter 3

Home is Where the Heart Is

Em sits on an examination table in a doctor's office. She's pointing out some irregularities on an ECG result to her physician. The ECG is displayed on a forty-inch video monitor mounted to the wall opposite the examination table. The results look like a series of wireframe peaks and valleys. The peaks are the same distance apart save for two. Em's fixating on the two unusually wide valleys.

"See, there and there." She says, concerned.

The doctor doesn't seem worried. "Benign. Hearts just do this sometimes. It's stress. I'd tell you about the heart's secondary and tertiary pacemakers but I know who I'm talking to..."

"I know you know. I also know you know an expert opinion is therapy in itself."

"Ever think of seeing an actual therapist?" the doctor gibes.

"Just load me up with valium and roll me on my side."

Doc drops the irony now. "What's adding to your stress you think?"

"No idea."

"Not a certain political actor who's been all over the news of late?"

"Burgess' exposure isn't helping, no."

"What's stressing you more, what she did to *Em the nurse* or what she did to *Em the cop*?"

"Harassment charges come with the territory."

"So the former." The doc changes his tone to reassuring. "She'll go down sooner or later. Even us self-involved docs noticed her sleaze. In the meantime, I'm putting you in touch with a great clinician I know. She specializes in cognitive behavioral therapy, perfect for a person like you who'd rather pop a pill than vent."

"Melatonin smart guy. Brain makes it after dark. Comes over the counter when it doesn't."

Doctor laughs. "Be that as it may, I'm still referring you to a therapist. You won't go, but I'm still referring you."

Em looks bored with the formalities all a sudden. She attempts a one-eighty on the doctor/patient professionalism maintained to now. She pulls the stirrups out of the examination table she sits on, caresses them a little suggestively, then pulls the doctor closer by his belt.

"You know what else is therapeutic?"

"You're changing the subject," he says without stopping the seduction. "I could lose my license..."

"You need to lose something else." She unbuckles his belt.

"Ah, fuck it."

They start kissing, soap opera style, *MWACK! MWACK! MWACK!*

Then...

THUMP! A sound is heard from outside the rear office door. The two lovers pause.

Doc gazes into his patient's eyes, hint of a frown. "Looks like the fruit of these little escapades has stopped by to ensure she remain an only child."

EM AND HER HUSBAND/PHYSICIAN, Robert 'Bob' Gray, enter their kitchen through a door with two signs over it. One sign says,

Appointment in Progress. Absolutely do NOT Enter.

It's placed next to a little red light that turns off as the two exit. The other sign reads,

Waiting Room.

It's next to a little green light that's currently off.

Bob and Em's daughter Leigh is making a toaster waffle and coffee in the kitchen. Bob greets his daughter with a hug.

"Hi honey." He puts a hand to her forehead. "Pale. Get more vitamin D."

Leigh reacts as though patronized and loved at the same time. "I'm fine dad, walked *all* the way here."

Em gives her daughter's face the same once-over Bob did, only at a distance. It *is* slightly paler than her usual almond. No sweat, hair is dry and flowing. She's also wearing a light hoodie. Em turns to the digital thermometer. *Outdoor* reading is eighty-five degrees at seventy-eight percent humidity.

"That'll get you a good dose," Bob says, assured. He grabs the barely filled coffee decanter and starts pouring.

"You robbin' the pot old man!" Leigh protests.

"My pot to rob." The green light next to the waiting sign comes on. Bob notices. "Back at it." He kisses his daughter on the forehead, his wife on the cheek, and heads back into his home office.

Em moves closer to Leigh. "Making yourself at home?" She lifts herself up on her tippy toes to kiss her standing daughter's forehead hello. Leigh leans down to accommodate her.

"This isn't my home?"

"I don't know, is it? Haven't had to cover your rent in a while."

"I got an arrangement."

"I don't like the sound of that. I'll tell you what I think tomorrow."

"Why tomorrow?"

"Cuz that's when the uniform I got staking you out gives me his weekly report." Em smirks. "Unless *you* want to tell me."

Leigh looks her mother up and down, settles. Time to relent? Compromise? "I got a roommate... Please don't ask anything more. We're figuring things out."

"Like how to tell me *roommate* is a euphemism for *guy I'm shacking up with?*"

"*Shacking?*" Leigh mocks, "What makes you think it's a guy?"

"I'm not so old-fashioned you know. I've seen women in prison movies."

"Which?"

"*Chicago...*"

"*PFFT!* What makes you think it's a human?"

"Seen *Caligula* too..."

"What makes you think it's an entity of this Earth?

OOOWOOOWOOO!" She's splaying her fingers outward and jangling them.

"You think you can shake me my dear, like I'm some old prude. I'm still gonna change the subject... But I'm not so old-fashioned. First thing's *now*, bring your new friend over for dinner next Sunday."

"We'll see."

"Don't you have class?"

"Ooh, more than you if that's how you're gonna broach the subject. Week off. Practicums start Monday."

Em looks to one of her cop calling cards sitting on the kitchen island. She's looking at it but not reading it. "Listen, I want you to put in for a spot at an inner-city charter school, *New Era* maybe."

"I'm already assigned. 'Sides, why?"

"Because baby girl, I want you to see what life's really like for the people your professors put into little boxes."

"It's not as bad as you think, ma."

"*This is who you are... This is what you've experienced... This is how you see the world... This is your worth as a human being due the box we put you in...* am I about right?"

"Just gotta play the game until I get my degree."

"These guys sew the seeds of defeatism in people more than capable of solving their own problems and guilt in everybody else. It's all about capitulation for them. You know that right?"

"You're too cynical by half. Just gotta play the game mama."

"Hope so. I hear you under-twenty-fives have your heads on straight. I still want you to put in for a spot out of the 'burbs."

"Us *under-twenty-fives* are realists. I'll let you know."

"Thought I only ever gave the 'realist' speech to my rookies... You'll let me know next Sunday."

There's a knock at the door. Em goes to it looking a little confused.

Leigh semi-shouts after her, "I'll *let* you know."

Door opens. It's Bomn. He's looking far less preppy at the end of his first week as a detective, as is the trend at West Brandon Homicide. Looks like he's borrowed one of Tesque's suits.

"We taking your car today?" Em asks.

"Long day last. Thought I'd save you the mileage."

"*AHEM!*" Leigh clears her throat. "Or not? Since your car's free..."

Em smirks at Bomn, then turns to do the same to Leigh. "Wow. It's almost like the two of you were working as a little team to hatch this even littler plan." She spins again to double up that smirk at Bomn for good measure, then back to Leigh. She mock-relents. "Yes you can borrow my car sweetie."

Leigh jumps up to grab the keys from the hook next the door. "Thanks ma," she says as she moves past Em. "Thanks *pahdna,*" she says as she moves past Bomn. She gives his arm a slight squeeze as she passes. Bomn's receptive but otherwise nonchalant.

Em notices.

EM OPENS THE DOOR OF Bomn's car and looks at the passenger seat. While Bomn's out of eyeshot she holds her forearm up between the seat edge and the glove box. She's real quick about it. She gets in at the same time Bomn does and moves her seat forward a good five inches.

"That's better," she says. "Mind turning down the air conditioner?"

"Bomn starts the car and then hits a button repeatedly. Five illuminated bars next to a fan icon ratchet down to one.

Em appears to be looking absentmindedly out the window—in quiet contemplation. Then... "So, Leigh's seeing somebody new."

"She is?"

"Yeah. I'm going to meet him next Sunday. She's bringing him over for dinner."

"S—she is?"

"Yeah." She pauses an eight-and-a-half-month's pregnant pause. "Dress casual."

Bomn's silent a moment, then...

"Detective..."

"Save it for Sunday."

Chapter 4

Hostile Takeover

We're looking down at a forty-five-degree bird's eye angle—on the big block store from about six stories up. Would look like security camera footage if the altitude weren't so great and the aesthetics so natural. It's still dark. Time is between 4 a.m. and 5 a.m.

A black van comes creeping up to the front entrance, stopping over the yellow diagonal-stripe crosswalk running perpendicular the doors. The van starts rocking ever so slightly. Rocks a little more, then stops. The side door can be heard opening. Now nothing, no motion, no sound. Nothing for about five more seconds then... A large mass is thrown out and the door slides closed. The van rocks back and forth aggressively, ever so briefly, and peels away.

A likely security guard exits the storefront. He picks up speed as soon as he notices the mass. He gets to it and hunkers down beside trying to communicate. He rolls the mass over and we see that it's a body. Guard turns frantic. He runs back toward the storefront and we hear him yelling, muffled and inaudibly, into the open sliding door of the building.

A PHONE VIBRATES ON A nightstand, screen illuminating a half-second after the first rumble. Touch display reads,

5:42am
Caller:
Police Squad

Em's Fatbutt™ is also vibrating. It's paired to her phone. She rolls over onto her back, reaches for the watch, pushing *at* the answer button a few times before getting it. Bob grumbles as Em rolls the rest of the way around and out the bed in one fluid groggy stumble. She carries her phone with her into the ensuite bathroom.

We won't follow her in there. If you've seen one middle-aged cop on the toilet carrying out police business from her smart phone you've seen them all. Then...

Em exits the bathroom. "You up?"

"Evidently," Bob mumbles.

Em stomps her feet while letting out a guttural bellow ending with the shaking of the lower half of her face. Her lips flap over and over and a sound like *BWELLELLEL-LELLELL* comes out of them.

"Go back to bed," she says sweetly.

"Goddamn rituals," says Bob, already half unconscious.

EM AND BOMN WALK TOWARD the cordoned-off area of the store where the body lies. It's still a little dark, but the store's lights allow them to make out most of the scene. Two uniformed cops and the security guard who found the body are the only people there.

"This perimeter look wide enough to you?" Em asks.

"Nope," Bomn responds.

Em points at the officer closest her. "You *first?*"

"Yeah, Officer Geoffreys," says the first on the scene. "That's Officer Jaisons." He points to his partner.

"What for process?"

"Cordoned and pictures," First says.

She points at the body. "You make sure he's dead?"

First looks dumbfounded, worried. Silly question, but not so silly considering he didn't actually check.

"Relax officer. Keep going," Em demands.

"Just us and a couple security guards around... Oh, and a few stock-boys."

"Ok..." Em scans the place running some preliminary calculus of some sort. "Ok. You two head in with the guard and see if he'll let you have a look at surveillance. Better, see if you can get copies of any recordings. Bring 'em right back to us."

First nods and gestures for the guard to lead he and his partner into the store. They leave as Em and Bomn approach the body. Em stops, turns back to the two cops.

"Officers," she calls.

They turn, giving her their full attention.

"Ask nicely but ask *rightly.*"

Officers nod and enter the store where the employees wait.

Em reaches out to Bomn. "Hand me the flashlight would ya?"

He does. She takes it, clicks it on and shines the beam all over the corpse-turned-supine by the security guard.

"Is that what I think it is?"

Corpse is wearing a full-head mask. Mask's of a pig. Em moves the light down to a discoloration on the corpse's chest and leans closer to it. It's a sign hanging around the corpse's neck that reads:

Pock-Mark Pigs Get Stuck.

"Shit. *WAMN*," Em says.

"*WAMN*," Bomn reiterates.

"*With Any Means Necessary.*"

"I know."

She starts patting down the clothes of the victim. He's wearing a fairly common black tracksuit. "Militant protest group." She turns the pockets inside out. Empty. "*Protest* being their choice of words."

"Oh, I know," insists Bomn. "Real kid gloves with the DA."

"This is their MO. Murder notwithstanding."

"You're just talking to yourself at this point..."

"*You need to get more sleep Detective Gray,*" Em mocks. "*No shit Detective Gray.*" She stands up. Looks slightly annoyed. "Dammit. You ask those guys if they called for an evidence tech?"

"Nope."

"*Dammmmiiit.* I really wanna know who's under that mask."

"Me too."

"We should probably call for the tech..."

"Protocol..."

"I ever tell you you have to be a *realist* on this job Bomn?"

"Every day."

"I ever tell you you have to be a *pragmatist* too?"

A moment of useless hesitation, then... "Hell with it. I'm having a look." She hunkers back down.

Bomn moves between the store surveillance camera and Em. She reaches toward the head of the body and begins furling the mask upward, real ginger. She rolls it higher and higher and higher... Until...

"*Mother father figure!*" Bomn blurts in shocked realization.

"*Mother fucker!*" says Em in the same shock.

It's Bertrand Park. His face is contorted in a painful last expression. There are ligature marks around the front of his neck.

"That's..."

They both, slowly, look up to the Park-Mart sign.

"We have to keep this quiet as long as we can," Em says, not looking away from the sign. "Once the *h'archy preservation society* gets ahold of this we'll be lucky if the Major lets us talk to each other. Real. Quiet."

THE STORE'S A CARNIVAL. THERE are media everywhere—photo, video, mouths... Reporters are shouting at anyone in earshot from behind the perimeter tape where a few inside are actually idiot enough to answer. Major K.J. Glynn—rumor has it the *K* stands for *King*, literally, *King*—is on the scene barking orders next to a tinted-glasses-wearing bureaucrat at his hip.

Morning shoppers and gawkers are on the scene too, pushing up against the media pushing up against the perimeter. Nobody thought to tell store staff and shoppers to stay home. Drones buzz through the air. It's chaos.

Tesque is there of course, the only professional in an

administrative position professional enough to be disgusted by the shit show. He, Em, and Bomn half and half and half it as ME techs take Park's body away. "I want the two of you out of here before anyone knows you're leads," the sergeant orders. "Apparently somebody tipped off Charles Reime so get to him while his head's still full of fact not rumor."

Em listens to her superior as she surveys the chaos. "Do me a favor," she says. "Lend us your unmarked."

"Son of a bitch!" Tesque shouts.

Em looks at the sergeant stone-faced and waiting.

Without even acknowledging Em, Tesque swaps out the keys and makes a beeline for The Major and Bureaucrat approaching. He gestures a *go go* motion at the lead investigators as he moves away to intercept.

THE DETECTIVE INCHES THE unmarked closer to the large gate of Reime's even larger estate. It's slow going. Some members of the media, gawkers too, and a perfect combination of both, are already on the scene. Cars are abandoned all along the shoulders of the estate entrance as the day's opportunists walk right down the middle of the mile-long driveway.

"It's like a Woodstock of bloodlust," Em observes.

"So, Woodstock 99," Bomn says. "I can't imagine what tipped off Reime..."

"Ha, partner. Alright, we're using the cowcatcher."

Em flips on the berries and cherries. She drips the siren a little. *WHOOP! WHOOP!*

Seeing the glare, and without missing a beat, professional and amateur photographers alike turn and start shooting away at the cop car. *Never know?* Some of the less experienced photogs even have their flashes on. Scene looks like a battle between camera flashes and cop lights.

Em glances over at Bomn's muted, non-descript attire strobing away against the cameras. "And you're not even wearing your good suit."

She jumps out of the car and hustles toward the gate.

WE'RE ON THE FRONT DOOR of the Reime residence. Door opens to greet Em standing there. Her hair's matted, skin clammy and flushed. The top button of her blouse is undone. She's holding her suit jacket folded over her left arm too. Looks like she's been hiking.

A brick wall of a man is standing on the other side of the entrance to greet her. Guy looks like he fell out of every eighties action movie poster. He smiles cordially.

Em smiles back. "Detecti— Shi—orry." She unfolds her suit jacket, hangs it out at the man and shakes it, revealing her police badge hanging from the breast pocket. "Detective—"

"Detective Eminence Gray," the man anticipates.

"I take it Sergeant Tesque—"

Big man interrupts again. He's clearly a professional, clearly has authority too, but he's overzealous in the most incongruous of ways. Here's why... "You were head of the OR at Brandon General," he beams. "You pressed for my mom to be moved up the case list for her bowel resection."

Em's taken aback but realizes what's happening. "Triage," she says matter-of-factly. "She was likely critical—"

"By all accounts you saved her life Detective."

"Well, the operating team deserves—"

"I understand they came down on you pretty hard for

that decision. Some muckety politician's kid had to wait an extra day for his tonsillectomy."

Em looks at her biggest oak tree of a fan quizzically. He notices.

"Ah geez..." he gushes, puts out a hand. "Gabriel Hack. I'm handling security for Mr. Reime." He welcomes Em in. "Pardon my lapse in professionalism but I'd be remiss if I didn't extend my and my family's appreciation for what you did."

"Well... I appreciate the appreciation," she says fumfering a little. She plays the same game as Hack, trying to muster some professionalism. "My partner is parking the—"

"Gabe!" shouts a voice, haughty and self-assured. "You're not letting one of those vultures into our home are you?"

A stern-looking young woman enters the foyer staring daggers at Em. Hack acknowledges her and hops to it.

"Ms. Reime, this is Detective Eminence Gray. She's the lead investigator in Mr. Park's murder."

The woman's demeanor changes hardly at all. "*Hmmm.*" She looks a look of scoffing at Em. "Who is the detective Miss Gray?"

Em reacts as anyone would fawned over then resented in the span of a minute. "Pardon me?"

The woman smirks. "Am I to *just* deduce the fact that you're here in an investigative capacity? Or, do you not have some credentials?"

Em maintains a now no longer due decorum. She reaches for her badge in the re-furled jacket as Hack tries to apologize for Ms. Reime's behavior... By proxy... By body language. Ms. Reime notices.

"Oh, Miss Gray," she faux-relents. "I do apologize for

my expectation of professionalism, but I've been through so much this morning, and we all grieve in our own unique way, don't we?"

Em smiles in a tight-lipped, left side of the mouth higher than the right side, kinda way that makes clear the girl's condescension is not lost on her. "I take it, Ms. Reime, you're suggesting that should one be sufficiently bereaved at Mr. Park's passing, we forgive her her boorish manner and complete lack of social graces? Unique grieving processes and all?"

Haughty demeanor drops away. "What are you intimating?" the girl asks coldly.

"Just drawing a careful inference. To reassure you I'm more than capable of doing my job." Em smiles again, albeit more symmetrically.

Ms. Reime smiles back in a facile, slightly flustered way. She turns and marches off down the hallway back in the direction she came. "Father is this way," she huffs, leading everyone several paces out front.

"You're welcome for any assurances..." Em whispers.

Hack grins at the remark as the two follow Ms. Reime toward the office. Office is slightly to the right of the end of a long hall, at the other end of the foyer, opposite the main entrance. The girl keeps a steady pace, seemingly just to keep a constant distance from Em. She walks right on by the office entrance gesturing limply at it as she passes. Disappears around the corner. Hack knows the layout anyway. He and Em get to the end of the hall and he motions for the detective to wait a moment.

"I'm just going to slip in and inform Mr. Reime of your arrival. Please have a seat."

Em sits on a bench outside the double office doors as Hack moves through them.

"Gabriel couldn't say out loud what his body language was attempting," says a voice up to now outside of Em's eyeline. "But I can."

The detective turns to see a confident, pleasant-looking and plane-dressed woman standing off to her left. She's holding a glass of water.

"I apologize for Sydney's behavior," says the woman. "I saw you coming up the drive. You look like you could use this." She hands Em the water and sits next to her. Em drinks. Thirstily. The woman continues accounting for the girl's behavior—*Sydney* evidently. "Sydney really has a good soul. Her father raised her according to what he called *the deserted island principle*." She takes the empty water glass off Em's hands, as any good servant would. "The game: imagine yourself on a deserted island. You have everything you've ever had save for your material wealth. What do you really have?" the woman gestures down the hall toward where Sydney disappeared. "Sydney found compassion. She also found superciliousness, hence the quibbling over professionalism. It's good for her that you pushed back like you did."

"I have a daughter near her age," Em acknowledges. "I wish she'd assert herself like that once in a while. Compassionate as hell. Intelligent as hell. But just gonna play the game..."

"But she asserts herself around you doesn't she?"

"*Oh yeah.* That's one thing about Leigh you can set your watch to."

"Then she'll be fine once she settles into a life with the people she truly cares about. If you have one job as the mother of your Leigh and I have one job as the mother of my Sydney, it's guiding them to this life."

"*Your Sydney?*" Em says in realization. "You're Mrs. Reime."

Mrs. Reime extends a hand. "Aylynn."

They shake in formal introduction as Hack reopens the office doors.

HACK WELCOMES EM INTO THE office, then looks to Charlie Reime. "Mr. Reime, Detective Eminence Gray."

Reime is leaning on the front of his large ornate desk, poised for greeting the detective. Em notices something immediately. Guy's white as a sheet and pore-sized beads of sweat have accumulated at his hairline. He looks calm in the sense that he's remaining still, but also looks like the tectonic plates that are his guts are about to start colliding any moment.

He extends a hand. "Detective Gr—"

WHEEEP! WHEEEP! WHEEEP! startles an alarm.

Em and Hack beeline for the office windows. As Em rushes past Reime, he, just barely in Em's line of sight, begins collapsing out the rest of it. No one seems to notice except...

"Charlie!" screams Mrs. Reime.

Hack's still paying attention to the source of the alarm. "Got him! Coming over the East wall."

Em turns to see Reime keeled over, Aylynn now crouched beside. She rushes to the couple. On instinct, she starts checking the CEO's vitals. She sits him against the front of his desk, opens his collar. He's out cold.

As the detective tends to him, she looks toward the window, an expression of concern on her face—not the kind you'd think.

. . .

REIME COMES TO. EM is monitoring his pulse at the wrist. There's a blood pressure monitor cuff attached to his other arm.

"What's all this?" he says, groggily.

"What this is, Mr. Reime, is a thready pulse and blood pressure all over the place." Em is trying to explain things while keeping Reime in a relaxed posture. "With adequate rest and relaxation, you'll soon be well enough to be a complete and total wreck."

Reime's a little more coherent and a lot more animated. He tries to get up. "These any means necessary tyrants... If they can get to Bertie..."

Em pats him on the shoulders in a *you need to take it easy* kinda pressure. "Feel that thump in your chest? That's your blood pressure bottoming out." she gestures both hands downward and Reime sinks back into a more relaxed posture. "Let's have a conversation. As we go, I want you to breathe in deeply over four seconds, hold for three, then out over four..."

Reime does this thoughtlessly, unquestioningly, like he's home from school with the flu and obliging his mom.

On the exhale, "You gotta get this guy."

"What we gotta do is find the perpetrator... Or perpetrators. We can do this a lot quicker with your—"

"Anything you need," Reime intercepts. "Name it."

"Breathe. Let's start with a few questions about the night you and Mr. Park were attacked."

Reime starts to sob. "Oh Bertie..."

Em rubs his shoulder. "When you're ready."

An agent of Hack's peeks in through the office door. Hack waves him in. He enters, accompanied by Bomn.

"Caught him trying to scale the East wall," says the agent.

Em looks to Bomn with a *this better be a joke* expression. She's taking her own pulse now. Bomn shakes his head.

"Some network reporter," adds the agent. "Got him in the wagon outside."

Em looks at Bomn with relief.

"We can take him in on trespassing," Bomn offers.

Reime shakes his head. "I'd rather you didn't."

"Only if he's your *guest* and he leaves of his own accord," Bomn says in compromise.

Reime nods to Hack. Hack nods to his agent. The agent leaves back for the door. As he goes, Em notices the heavy-duty carbine slung across his chest.

"Mr. Reime, these guys are paramilitary."

"Yes?" says Reime, seeking relevance.

"Well, there's a killer on the loose not a revolutionary army."

Reime gets it. "You must think me a real coward Detective..."

"Or, a man shooting squirrels in his attic with a bazooka. Heavy artillery like this could do more harm than good." Em turns to Hack. "No offense."

Hack waves it off in good humor as Reime tries lifting himself up again. Em helps.

"Hack's team's the best," Reime says as he rises. "They accompanied Bertie and I through China, Southern Asia, and Central America."

"Gap year?"

"Ha."

"Outsourcing."

"Yes," Reime says, leveling with Em. "Fact-finding... Look detective, it was clearly Bertie's and my fault but it wasn't our *doing* if you understand me correctly. Officious little department heads—thought they'd climb the ladder by saving us money—did what they thought they had to. It was always wrong."

Em nods, noncommittally. Changes the subject, "Now, about the night of the attack..."

Chapter 5

Carpetbaggers

Em gets to her desk at the start of shift. There's a folded piece of paper on it with 'Em' angling at her in Tesque's crappy scrawl.

SHE BARGES INTO HIS OFFICE, waving the note.

"What the hell is this?"

"Procedure. That I shouldn't have to remind you of. *We interview those last to see the victim alive...*"

"That's not what I meant. The conflict?"

"She personally requested the charges be dropped, remember?"

"Still a conflict of interest."

"Not if she's asking for you by name..."

EM INCHES THE CAR ALONG the boulevard in front of the massive corporate complex. She's driving slower than she needs, hunched over the wheel looking all around, taking in the scene. Picketers have filled the plaza.

Bomn's more about the police business of things. "Her manager said east of Building Four..."

Em's not listening. She's mesmerized by the enormity of the demonstration. "How many must be at the warehouses?" she asks herself.

"Huh?"

She's transfixed.

THE AUDITORIUM IS FILLED WITH striking nurses and non-union supporters.

At the front of the room is a stage, upon which sits a table, at which sit various Brandon Nursing Union board members. Janine Burgess, President, is at the center. Em's barely noticeable among the *hoi polloi* as audience.

It's Q&A time. A sister in solidarity, *Striker Shirley*, holds the microphone. She faces the board, having managed to move herself all the way to the front of the stage. She has the whole of the audience at her back as she talks directly to the union executives.

"I'd like to start by thanking all of you for your leadership and for sticking it to hierarchy!" she shouts.

There's some scattered hoots and cheers from the crowd.

"Solidarity! Whoo!" Shirley adds.

A few more cheers.

Em looks unimpressed. "Christ Shirl Girl..." She leans closer to the nurse to her right. "She's acting like she's gonna get airbrushed out the union calendar if the seal between her lips and Burgess' asshole lets in even a faint of a fart of daylight..."

Nurse to Em's right chuckles.

Striker Shirley goes on, "I think we could all use a reminder of what we're fighting for Nina."

Burgess turns to her colleagues at her right, they nod back and forth. She turns to the left, same exchange. She rises, bows solemnly at the crowd.

"Thank you Shirley."

Shirley looks like she's going to swoon. Burgess looks like she's squinting real hard to read Shirley's name tag.

Burgess continues, "This government of ours, they talk a good game about the importance of healthcare. About supporting our nurses. But they don't *play* that game. They also talk a good game about their prized rainy-day fund, a product of their *impeccable fiscal responsibility*. Well, we all know how fast rain turns to slush in the hands of this government. I say we can't afford to let that rainy day fund turn into yet another of their slush funds. Not when so many hard-working nurses are burning themselves out and so many of our sick are suffering for it! They have a rainy-day fund, well I say it's raining now! We're going to keep fighting for that money to cure our sick, ease our people's suffering, and birth our future." Now Burgess really goes for broke. "We've been bringing the rain for their rainy day for weeks now and trust me on this my sisters, when it comes to the BNU, when it rains it pours!" She has them on their feet. "Well, we've brought the flood. Oh yes we have! And now we're going to bring the thunder! Solidarity!"

The whole crowd erupts in applause and cheers... everyone but Em.

Crowd settles.

"Well, if there are no more ques—"

"I have a question," Em informs.

"Y—yes?" Burgess says, taken aback.

"The pomp and poetry notwithstanding... Because it

doesn't... I'm glad you brought up the concept of funds." Em pauses a second, looks to her colleagues, back to Burgess. "I'm glad you brought that up Nina because, as you know, our local raised nearly two-million dollars in strike funds the last few years. We scrimped and we saved. We fundraised, invested. Our kids even collected beer cans at the local music festivals."

"And?" asks Burgess, a little impatient.

"*And?* We've been on strike for three weeks now and haven't seen a dime of that money. We did everything according to the finance committee's requirements. When are they going to release those funds?"

It's a simple question, a serious one too considering these nurses' circumstances, but this is where it gets really really weird for Em and her fellow healers...

Burgess and the rest of the board, in response to this question, pause for a second or two, then...

"Well, if there are no more questions..." Burgess says, looking a thousand yards through Em.

The board rises to match the already-standing Burgess. They all start shuffling toward the exit. Lois Walsh, fellow nurse and person we're about to see shares a duopoly on backbone with Eminence Gray, stands up among the confused crowd.

"Excuse me! Em has a valid question and you owe her an answer. You owe us all. Where's the strike fund?"

Again, nothing from the board but...

"If there are no more questions, then..."

The board moves for the exit even faster. Several in attendance smell the rat there to be smelled and start yelling and jeering. Others are hesitant to criticize the higher-ups. Striker Shirley looks like the dissonance is about to tear her in two.

All are on their feet, some demanding answers, some demanding silence from those demanding answers. All but Em. She sits, stone-faced and pensive.

Burgess is gone.

BOMN'S BEEN TALKING TO A distracted partner for several seconds now. "...the lead on this."

"What?" she says, coming out of her daze.

"I'll take the lead."

"Why?"

"Your history with a potential witness."

"What history's that?"

Bomn looks at her imploringly. *Who ya kiddin' Em?*

"That ain't the half of our history partner."

Bomn looks at her like he wants that gap filled.

"Let's just say, she's the reason I became a cop."

Bohm has a second or two look of contemplation, then understanding. He mouths the word *oh*.

Em softens. "Thanks Jack, I appreciate you looking out. Oh, by the way, I was thinking..."

"What about?"

"Why don't you take the lead?" She grins.

"Great idea..."

Em's focus goes back to the bustle of the complex. "Gawd I wish I didn't have to be here."

"Why *are* you here?"

"Burgess asked for me..."

"I'LL MAKE THIS CLEAR UP front Detective, I never asked for you." We're in Burgess' mobile-home-as-executive-suite. She's about a third paying attention to the cops and about two-thirds reading some documents while altering figures on a whiteboard. She directs one-hundred percent of her rapid-fire verbiage at Em. "I have no interest in discussing anything with the cop who made my life a living hell for near a year."

"I made *your* life a living hell?" Em says.

"*Em*," Bomn reprimands in hush.

Burgess flips a page in her paper-clipped documents and reaches to the board. She wipes out a dollar value to the right of the words 'Entry Wage:' and writes in a new figure. It reads,

Entry Wage: $22.25

By the way, Burgess' trailer's gotta be twelve-hundred-square-feet and is lavish as hell. Only thing drab is the whiteboard in the living room portion hogged out to function as office. Desk and information technology sit everywhere, along with various other furnishings that are state-of-the-art boutique nonsense.

Her words are back on Em now. "The fact is, my advisors informed me that because of our past, your department would be sending a proxy. They also informed me that this could drag these proceedings out far longer than necessary. I simply can't afford to be in ongoing meetings with police over routine formalities. I'm in the process of standing with near three million Amerikan workers fighting for their livelihoods—"

"But not *your* livelihood?" Em interrupts. "Never had a taste for the warehouse floor? I'd say it's not in a nurse's temperament, though you were never one of those either."

"*Em!*" Bomn says, still hushed but piercing.

Burgess must have managed to put a lid on the resentment brewing because she only looks about a tenth as bitter as she is. She still can't help but grimace a little as she responds. "Oh yes, *Burgess the carpetbagger*," she says. "I still had to get elected Em. You chose me remember?"

"Before you stole our living."

"It was expansion of union infrastructure. Routine, not-to-mention necess—"

"Two million dollars raised in four years. Ear-marked for a strike fund. We busted our asses."

"Strike funds *and such*."

"You slimy politish—"

"Em!" Bomn says this in no kind of hush.

Em relents. She leans back and gestures for Bomn to take over.

Burgess isn't finished with Em though. "I needed to get these proceedings over with so I requested the lead investigator. Unfortunately that was you."

"Famous last words..."

"Is that a threat?" asks Burgess.

"No," Em insists. "Just a comment on the fact that you always have to get the last word. You're *famous* for it."

Burgess is preparing some last words when...

"*Ms. Burgess*," Bomn says in a tone meant to catch her attention. Redirect works. Burgess turns to the junior detective, bowing limply in receptivity. He proceeds. "Did you happen to see any suspicious persons on the night of your and Mr. Park's speaking engagement? Before, during, or after? Anyone who looked out of the ordinary?"

"Besides the boy who accosted Mr. Park and Mr. Reime?"

"He's been ruled out as a suspect," Bomn offers.

"Then no. I can't say that I did."

"What about the rest of the entourage?" Em asks.

"Excuse me?"

"The muppies with the first-year mindset who follow you wherever you go. The forty-something revolutionaries with the signs and the mouths…"

"They care about justice, detective. I care about justice. We're like moths to a flame. The flame of injustice brought us to that event, not each other. I don't know them."

"I didn't ask you if you *knew* them," Em clarifies. "I asked you if you thought them suspicious?"

"I think them heroic, Detective. I couldn't be more heartened to see the fruits of our wonderful educational systems taking such a keen interest in the world around them."

"Pretty old fruit…" Em whispers to Bomn. "Do you think Mr. Reime's attacker heroic?"

"I think his attacker… Misguided," says Burgess.

"And quite impressionable. All this talk of revolution on your part. Rising up, uniting, fighting the powers that be and what have you."

"I'm sorry, are you accusing me of incitation?"

"I can assure you Ms. Burgess," Bomn interjects. "Detective Gray is accusing you of nothing of the kind." He finds his place among his mental script for how to play *vengeful cop/fish out of water cop* and continues. "Ms. Burgess, did Mr. Park confide anything in you the night in question? Mention anything that suggested fears, concerns, apprehensions? Anything that may inform us as to who the perpetrator might be? Be as specific or as broad as you wish."

She shakes her head. "No. What little we spoke he was his usual self."

Em's exercised by Burgess' use of *usual self.* "What are your overall impressions of Mr. Park?" she asks.

"Don't tell anyone I ever said this, detectives, but for someone who stands for everything I oppose, he's one of the kindest people I've ever known." Burgess looks almost wistful. Then... "*Reime* on the other hand... What about him?"

Em smirks. "Wouldn't that be nice. Your biggest political opponent guilty of murdering your second."

"Not necessarily what I meant."

Em turns off the smirk. Goes rote. "Did anything about Mr. Reime's behavior that evening strike you as odd or suspicious?"

"Just a tension between Reime and Park. Really, more a general distaste the latter seemed to be directing at the former."

"Well, we can't discuss Mr. Reime's relationship to this investigation at present. However, we'll keep your observations in mind," Em assures.

"So you haven't ruled Reime out as a suspect?"

"What makes you say that?" Em asks, genuinely curious.

"Well, as Detective Bomn made clear, Mr. Park and Mr. Reime's assailant *has* been ruled out as a suspect." Bomn's head lowers as Burgess continues. "Apparently you *can* discuss his relationship, so I figure if a potential suspect's been ruled out, they're fair game?"

Em looks to Bomn. "Detective?"

Bomn lifts his head, contrite. "I shouldn't have said that."

"Well that explains that," Em says boisterously. "I think we have all the information we need. The department thanks you for your time Ms. Burgess."

Em and Bomn rise ready to leave. Burgess gestures for them to wait.

"One more thing Detective Gray. I fully intend for this to be our last meeting. Pardon me if I can't give you the benefit of any doubt, but I don't want those machinations of yours, that there be any improprieties involved in our union's spending—for instance—jeopardizing our strike efforts. I've arranged for our accountants to release to you complete records of our funds in reserve, investments, deposits from members and donors—names redacted of course—our spending, etc." Burgess affects a political tone once more—as though she'll go into some sort of withdrawal if she doesn't. "These records will prove our strike fund is robust, capable of matching eighty percent of our workers' incomes for at least the next four months, where all spending is above board."

Em smiles. "Appreciate it."

"You should have the first of the documents by this time tomorrow."

"Perfect." No irony.

"I will be sending your Major a copy of these documents as well."

"Naturally."

Em nods. Bomn nods too. They start walking toward the exit. As they go, Bomn looks distantly hesitant *again*. Perturbed *again*.

"Detective..."

Em frowns.

IT'S A ROUTINE MEETING OF Brandon Police detectives, Detective Sargent, as well as any uniforms involved with robbery/homicide cases not currently participating in the field. The only break from routine is the presence of The Major and his bureaucrat.

Incidentally, Em has taken to wearing a button on her lapel that reads the following,

-5

The button turns out to be a fixture for the remainder of these proceedings.

Tesque's standing to the left of a lectern at the front of the room. He's got his elbow on it but he doesn't need the leverage. "Alright, high profiles first for a change." He looks to the Major and bureaucrat with some reproach. "What's the rundown on Park?"

Bomn goes first. "Since his wife died, he's lived like a virtual recluse. Work and home."

Em takes the baton. "Every day but Sunday his driver walks him to his town car. 5:15 am on the button." She starts reciting from some notes. "Office from roughly 5:45 am to 3 pm. In-car forty-five minutes. Driver walks him back up to his penthouse upon arrival home."

"No driver on Sunday?" Tesque asks.

"No."

"What's he up to on Sundays?" Tesque follows.

"Never leaves his penthouse," says Bomn.

"Shit."

"Not shit," says Em.

"No shit?"

"Guy never leaves his penthouse *save* for a thirty-minute walk around, then through, the Grove. Every Sunday. Same path. Every Sunday."

Tesque livens a little. "Gotta be when he was grabbed then. Let's knock on some doors and get any department surveillance for that time of day."

"Hold it," says Em. "I didn't say same *time* every day. I said same *path*."

"Guy this Kantian doesn't do everything according to an invariant schedule?"

"He times his walks for the sunset, comin' up west through the park pass. It was he and his wife's little tradition."

"Alright then," Tesque sums up. "Get a goddamn astronomer in here and let's figure out Park's itinerary."

"Just waiting on the techs to clean up department surveillance," Bomn offers.

"Good. Check with *Rec* and other municipal departments too. Never know."

A plain-clothed cop volunteers for this by gesture.

"Good good." Tesque moves everyone along. "*Ins* and *outs* on the Park case so far. Saint?"

Again, Bomn goes first. "Saint's been traveling the country all month hosting hot-button speaking engagements. Caught the red eye to Boston two days before the murder. Gone."

"Burgess?"

"Nah," says Em. "Fact that *WAMN*'s boilerplate is all over the crime scene implicates her. They follow her around like little militant puppy dogs. She wouldn't be so stupid to conspire murder with people this close to her."

"Maybe alibi?" asks Tesque. "*Of course I didn't do it. Only an idiot would orchestrate a murder knowing the murderers would directly implicate 'em!*"

Em cracks an ironic smile. "Wow, look who's watching *Basic Instinct* for the plot... As much as I'd love to see Burgess go down for this, negative motive. Park is Burgess' white whale. She's been dreaming of collectivizing Park-

Mart out from under him since *my* union days. Park's death hurts her politically. She lets nothing hurt her politically."

"Reime?"

"Reime?" Bomn says. "Now Reime's an anomaly. *Motive*: his good standing in the company is starting to falter. He and Park may have had a falling out. Getting Park out of the picture keeps Reime where he is, maybe even shoots him up the ladder. *Opportunity*: frequent direct access to Park. Also knows his every move, his patterns, his vulnerabilities. *Means*: he's the top executive of Park's. Endless resources."

"So, what's the anomaly?"

"He's really fucking scared he's getting it next," Em offers. "He's more a recluse than Park now and we estimate he's already spent eighty grand in private security."

"Small price for misdirection."

"Doubt it. Reime's scared. Plus, he really loved the old guy."

Tesque looks a little annoyed. "Your psychologizing notwithstanding Em... Because it doesn't... He's our best suspect after the *WAMN* brigade. Keep an eye on him."

Ahem goes Bureaucrat. Major hops to it.

"An unobtrusive eye," Major insists.

Tesque looks a lot annoyed. "Alright, *WAMN in.* Reime *in.* Saint *out.* Burgess?" Tesque gestures to Em.

She shakes her head. "I wish, but I say no."

"*Maybe?*" Em appears to find this agreeable. Bureaucrat looks uneasy. Major shakes his head at Tesque. Tesque looks back at Em, smirks. "That's a definite *maybe.*" He reaches over to the lectern and grabs another pile of documents. "Moving on. Bob's Liquor..." Bureaucrat and the Major get up to leave. "...You heard the clerk didn't make it, so it's been reclassified a homicide..."

Major and Bureaucrat pass by Bomn and Em.

"Dickles," the junior detective says in a whisper.

Em baps him on the arm in an *I'm starting to like this guy* gesture. Not to say she doesn't like Bomn, she's just liking him a lot more.

IT'S THE DETECTIVE'S BULLPEN. EM sits at her desk across from Bomn's. She tosses a wad of paper at him, getting his attention.

"So, my daughter write those trite term papers because you've been helping her, or do you go around sounding like the pope of post-modernism because you've been reading those trite term papers?"

"Just gotta play the game mama..."

"Ugh. You don't, *cop*. Also, don't ever call me *mama* again or I'll make you a mama, understand?"

"Nobody understood that."

Em looks like she's confused, herself. "Yeah, that made no sense. It was meant to be emasculating."

"*Sexist.*" Bomn says, flip.

Em tries to affect her best Nigel Tufnel voice, "*So what? What's wrong with being sexist?*"

"Oh for two mama..."

"*PFFFT!*" Em goes. It was a playful *PFFFT!* Though.

Bomn notices Em's -5 button. He gestures to it. "What's with that?"

"I'll tell ya sometime..." she smirks.

"Alright kiddos," Tesque says, appearing out of nowhere. "It begins. Who's the bad guy?"

Bomn shifts back to professional. Real abrupt. "Well..." He sits up in his seat. "We've ruled out Reime and Park's attacker."

Em doesn't shift back to professional. Talks nonetheless. "Mr. Milkshake got himself apprehended the Friday prior and was caged until the judge got in on Monday."

"Long weekend."

"Tuesday."

Tesque is flipping through a hot sheet as his detectives speak. Gets to the page of relevance. "Don't be so sure. DA dropped the case second she heard."

"Of course she did!" Em says, disgusted. "Establishment trying to keep people who think they're taking down the establishment from noticing DA's the establishment. If this guy were holding *Fuck DA Givens!* rallies, he'd be in fed-pen, no bail, and everyone he knows *n'* grandma'd be brought in on *conspiracy to commit the counseling of mischief.* Nice favor Givens did him in the end though..."

"How's that, Em?"

"Denying him an alibi."

"You're talking about him walking on alibi like he didn't do it," Tesque says.

"Exactly. Let's go roust him." Em stands to get her coat.

"Who ya roustin'?" asks a detective entering the pen. He's moving swiftly toward Em and Bomn.

"*Milkshake,*" she says lifting her coat off the rack. She lets it hover a second.

"Was in jail."

"Charges were dropped," Em challenges.

"That's why I'm looking for you. Shithead got himself arrested again." The detective shakes a file that apparently proves this.

"You're kidding?" Bomn says grabbing it.

"Threw a brick through a McDonald's window," the detective insists.

"Vandalism?" asks Bomn vigorously flipping through the pages.

"*Theft*," the detective laughs. "Stole the brick from a construction site. Got him on CCT."

"How long was he in?" Em asks.

"Across your homicide."

She puts her coat back on the rack and sits down. She looks at Bomn, aggravated. "Did we just buy a pair of shoes to go shoe shopping again?"

She stands right back up.

"Alright, we need better communication around here! Transparency, dix. It's how we do the job."

She sits back down, slouched.

She stands right back up... Again.

She grabs her coat, looks back to Bomn. "You call me if that surveillance comes in. I got a lunch."

Chapter 6

Union Ain't the Same as Solidarity

The entry corridor of *Local #7491* headquarters is lined with portraits of past and present local executives. Em's looking at the current president, her old friend Lois Walsh. A small bronze placard is tacked into the bottom of the frame. It reads:

> *Lois Walsh*
> *President 2218-*

She strolls a few portraits over, real leisurely, no rush. She stops, leans closer to the portrait in front of her. Placard reads:

> *Eminence Gray*
> *President 2207-2212*

IT'S THE SAME AUDITORIUM EM confronted Burgess in over the funds. Burgess is even standing atop the same part of the same stage, yammering on in the same way, next to the same board members. The only difference is, this is a meeting between just the board and the executives of each local.

Each local has its own gala table decked out in fine linen and place settings. At the center of each table is a placard with the number of the respective local printed on it. The nurses at table 7491 listen as Burgess speaks. The word *hierarchy* is said numerous times.

To clarify, all but Em are listening. She's distracted, shuffling, looking in the opposite direction of the stage when she rises, abrupt. "Excuse me ladies. I'll be right back." She moves for the back exit.

A board member is leaving at the same time. Em smiles at her and holds the door.

THE ENTRY/EXIT OF THE headquarters' washrooms are those open-concept wide-hallway deals. The kind that lead in about twenty feet, zig left about ten, then zag back into the washroom another few. You know, the kind to keep people from bumping into each other coming in and out or from having to reach out for grimy door handles. The layout works just fine for Em as she comes flying around those zigs and zags completely unencumbered, driving her pantsuit like it's a rally car. She moves out the last zig and turns left, disappearing out of sight. The board member she held the door for follows shortly after, putting her suit jacket back on as she leaves. Getting the coat over her shoulders she realizes something's missing. She glances down to her pocket, confirms some fact to herself, then heads back into the can.

· · ·

A KEYCARD SWIPES OVER A digital panel outside the Finance Committee file room door. The little red light on the panel turns into a little green light and the massive aluminum door goes *AYNK!* then clicks.

Door opens and Em walks through, tucking the keycard/identification into her breast pocket. Card says,

Teresa Mills, Finance Committee Chairperson

Em tracks along a row of file cabinets, stopping on one that says,

Auxiliary Accounts

Drawer opens, fingers skim along the file folders stopping on,

BNU #7491

She pulls it and starts flipping through the pages. Flipping... Flipping... Stops. She whips a page out, scans the list of financial transactions on it. What's of most interest is the last pair of transactions at the bottom of the page,

HASH DEPOSIT-2478: $8,552 (BNU7491 Strike Fund)
Balance $1,972,845.27
HASH WITHDRAWAL-2479: $1,972,000.00 (PRO 828)
Balance $845.27

"There's our two mil..." she whispers. "But what the hell is *PRO 828*?"

Em has an epiphany. She moves to another part of the file room, to a grouping of file cabinets labeled,

Project Accounts.

Redo. Em's looking for another file of all files when... She makes a face like she's found what she's searching for. Reads quick.

"Mother fuck bucket!"

She scans around the rest of the room, stops, smiles. One last move: the photocopier.

EM SLIPS BACK INTO THE auditorium. She's hugging onto a large stack of bond booklets. She moves real quiet-like. Burgess isn't quiet at all though. She's still yammering on. *Hierarchy* this and *hierarchy* that...

Em's disseminating the material, beginning with the tables at the back of the room, moving forward. A dull murmur swells, louder and louder as more union members receive their copies. She gets to her local's table. By now the murmur has turned to clamor. She hands Lois a copy of the files and winks.

We can barely hear Burgess now and Burgess knows this. "...*Hierarchy*..." She stops the speech, curious. She speaks in a slight shout. "What? What's all this?"

Em hears Burgess from about a third of the room back and starts moving toward her briskly. As she moves along, she hands out the files more and more hastily and haphazardly.

Almost at the stage, she splits the stack of papers in two and tosses them in both directions, spreading her paper wings, feathers flyin'.

She stops at the stage, looks to the crowd—raises a hand holding the original of the culpabilitating documents. The crowd goes silent.

"What is this?" Burgess demands.

"This, Nina, is the answer to the question *what happened to our strike fund in '91?*" Em watches Burgess for a second. Burgess is cool. Appears to be waiting for the other shoe to drop. Could be a bluff. Em plays her cards. "Project 828."

Burgess shudders a little. She mouths the words *no, no, no* then... "Nope! No!"

Crowd starts to grumble. Em turns to them.

"She dumped eight million dollars of the money our locals raised into a state-of-the-art office complex just for her and her board cronies."

"Those files are confidential!" warns Burgess.

"Off limits to all but the head of *this union*. That's us, the collective! Or do you disagree?"

Burgess is shook, that's clear. There's always a hierarchy but you can't very well assert your position at the top of it when you've spent your whole political career denying the existence of it in order to maintain that position. Burgess gestures, pleading to the crowd. "I—it's standard expansion of infrastructure. As the union grows, so too does a demand for union resources."

"Fifty-two thousand dollars for a coy pond?" shouts an executive from the back.

Crowd erupts.

Em talks in the direction of the crowd but to Burgess. "Thirty-five below zero and we were marching for our lives! Thirty-five below zero and she didn't even have the courtesy to tell us she'd made us destitute by her own hand." She turns to Burgess for this one. "Our children were on that line!" Back to the crowd. "Destitute, while she sat in her..." Em reads from one of the pages. "... Thirteen-thousand-dollar *Hans Wagner* ergonomic swivel chair!"

Em looks to Lois. Lois looks to Em. Em nods. Lois has her opening...

"I call for an immediate emergency vote to dissolve the BNU board!" Lois shouts.

"Second!" says the president of Local #144.

"I call on the heads of each local to hold an emergency meeting to discuss criminal investigation of board actions!" Lois adds.

"Second!" says that same president.

"Lastly, I call on the board to demand the immediate resignation of Janine Burgess!"

Burgess swings her arms in a *don't be hasty* motion at the crowd. Crowd responds by breaking into a chant. *Re-Sign, Re-Sign, Re-Sign...*

Em looks at Burgess-as-BNU-president a last time. *"This* is solidarity."

EM'S MOVED TO A FRAMED group photo of her former local now. She appears wistful glancing at her sisters in healing.

"Em?"

She knows that voice. The detective turns to greet Lois.

"Lo."

They hug.

"Feelin' nostalgic?" Lois asks, slight suggestion in her voice.

"What do you have in mind?"

"Swamped. I was hoping you wouldn't mind doing lunch in the office... *Old times?*"

"What do you have on offer?"

"Half a tuna sandwich."

"Ha! *Old times* indeed."

"Old sandwich..."

. . .

LOIS SITS WITH HER FEET on her desk and Em sits with her feet on a chair identical to the one her butt's in, legs parallel to the floor. They're drinking white wine from those plastic champagne glasses while in mid-conversation. The uneaten tuna sandwich sits on the desk.

"It's a strange proposition, this job, isn't it?" says Lois. "Yell out to the world yer gettin' taken advantage of cuz ya can't band together to stand up for yourselves, then act surprised when some politician sleazes out of the earth to take advantage of ya cuz ya can't band together to stand up for yourselves..."

"We really rolled over and showed 'em our bellies didn't we?" Em laughs. "If there's one thing 'ol *hierarchy Hoffa* taught me, there's a difference between union and solidarity."

"Well, you taught her the real lesson."

"Did I? No criminal charges." Em looks at her little champagne glass, swishing the booze inside. "She has eighteen trailers across this city alone. Bigger than your house. Just to sit and watch picketers picketin'."

"Em..." Lois is starting to sound like Bomn.

Em gives Lois a *don't you say it* look.

Lois says it anyway, "Sleeping dogs."

"She's playing with billions this time."

"*Em...*"

"They got their kids on that line too." Em's feet on the floor now. She leans closer to Lois. "Weather's getting colder..."

Lois exhales, almost relenting. "Well?"

Em starts to grin. "Any connections you might have in the labor world Lois. Anyone with the goods on Burgess.

Anyone with the goods on anyone with the goods on Burgess. Put them in touch."

Lois exhales, definitely relenting. She tops up her glass.

Em grins a beaming grin at her.

PHONE RINGS AS EM EXITS the 7491 offices. She rushes to put her earbuds in and answer. She's pretty smooth about it too since she's now got her bulldog Lois on the case and is fixating on that. She's imagining all the incriminating evidence that's going to be pouring in—these imaginings taking up the bulk of her conscious processing—allowing for the efficiency and speed of neurological autopilot to drive those earbuds into her earholes like water to a sipping-straw.

"Em Gray's phone."

"*Detective!* Charlie Reime."

"How are you feeling?" She asks this not in detective mode yet.

"Still doing those breathing exercises. Listen, I've got something that might help with your investigation. I've set up meetings for you with our heads of security as well as Luce at our car service. They're open-ended appointments so stop by whenever you can."

"What are you thinking, Mr. Reime?"

"It's Charlie. They can corroborate when Bertie came and went and where. Most importantly, who came to see *him*."

Em's eyebrows raise and she nods a little to herself. *That's not bad thinking on his part...* "That's real good think-ing. Appreciate it Mr. Reime."

"*Charlie!*" he repeats, playfully insistent. "Just get this guy ok."

"Trying our best."

. . .

LEIGH'S HAVING LUNCH WITH BOMN. They sit at a large metal picnic table on the periphery of the school's playground, joined by a couple of Leigh's cooperating teachers. Children are playing all around too.

"So, does the FBI get involved?" asks one of the teachers.

"Oh, no," assures Bomn. "It's a straightforward homicide."

"But it's *so* high profile," says the other teacher.

"It's not a matter of national security—"

"He's one of the richest people in the world," the first teacher reminds.

Bomn smiles obligingly. "It's certainly high profile. N—no doubt about that—"

"You police?" A little girl asks this tugging at the detective's sleeve.

Bomn hunkers down to greet the little girl. "Yes I am."

"Dakota..." Little girl points to one of her friends off the way. "She says Mrs. Gray's husband isn't a police man. But I was right because you are."

"In a way, though not quite," says Bomn, little flustered.

"If you're not a police man then you shouldn't lie about it," the little girl observes. "It's illegal to lie about being a police man."

"Oh no, I just mean, we're not married."

Little girl peers carefully at Bomn. "So you two don't smooch? My mommy and daddy smooch. You smooch when you're married."

"Um..."

Bomn's eyes widen a little. Leigh smiles at him, waves her hand across the table toward the little girl, suggesting to

Bomn, *go on*. The little girl smiles a sly smile at Ms. Gray as Bomn searches for words.

"Bet you wish you were at a crime scene right now, huh?" the other teacher interjects.

Bomn takes a deep breath, prepares his next statement very carefully. "Well... You see... *Society*—"

"Bye!" The little girl runs off.

Leigh and the other teachers laugh stifled laughs. Bomn's phone rings.

"Hello," he answers. He registers the voice on the other end and whispers to Leigh, "Never thought I'd be so relieved to get a call from your mom..." He stands up, "Hey. Any news?" He's about to kiss Leigh goodbye but realizes the context. He pats her on the head awkwardly in lieu of that kiss goodbye. He realizes what he's done as he's walking away. *I'm sorry* he mouths back to her as he goes. She shakes her head. There's more stifled laughter.

"You listening rook?" Em's shouting comes through the earpiece.

"Yeah... Yup... Could you say that again, though—"

"Got an address for you to look into when you get back to the shop. Park's been there three times the last five weeks."

"Could be something."

"Could definitely be something. You should see the guy's day-to-day. He could teach the sun to rise. Then there're these sudden unscheduled trips? I'm texting the address."

"Listen," Bomn hastens. "Charles Reime's called me a couple times. Called the station too."

"Don't I know it," Em concurs. "These addresses are thanks to him."

"Guy's really... *Helpful*."

. . .

EM'S DRIVING. IT'S EASILY EIGHTY, eighty-five, percent of the job. She's still got Bomn on speakerphone. Real responsible. She's got a printout of the data she's texting to him at ten o'clock and her phone in-hand texting the address at two o'clock. Real not responsible. "I was thinking the same thing, partner..."

She looks up through the top of her windshield at a sign at the entrance of a gated compound. Sign reads,

Hack-King Security

EM AND HACK WALK ALONG a shooting range at the rear of the compound. Highly proficient paramilitary agents are doing the obvious: shooting proficiently. Then...

"Agent!" barks Hack.

The trainee-addressed spins, firearm in hands. He immediately realizes the point of the test, looks down in disappointment. *Shit.*

"Where's that muzzle?"

"Sorry," the trainee says.

"Where's that muzzle?"

"Away from friendlies at all times. Sorry boss. It's clear a' rounds..."

"That gun is always loaded! You get me?"

The Agent nods. Hack holds out his hand. The Agent pulls a loonie from his pocket and drops it in Hack's open palm. Palm closes.

Hack and Em walk on.

"New guy," Hack explains. "Rough around the edges but a quick learner. He won't do that again."

"Rooks *are* quick aren't they. Just don't introduce 'em to your daughter."

Hack chuckles. "What was that, detective?"

Em waves the comment off. *Never mind.* She stops at an unoccupied range station. "Whoa. Look at these." What she's attending to is a plethora of ostentatious weapons of various sorts, lying next to their respective ammunition.

"Welcome to Hollywood," Hack says, waving his hands over the novelty weapons. "Wanna give one a try?"

Em's intrigued. Makes a *may I?* gesture. Hack nods and she picks up the Desert Eagle. She drives in the clip, observes the gun's mechanisms a second, comprehends, then readies the weapon to fire.

Aims... Aims... *BANG!*

She can barely handle the recoil. Round hits the silhouette of the target in the right shoulder.

"Too much gun for me," she chuckles.

"Me too!" Hack laughs. "Things just a goddamn ornament. But you'd know better than anyone how many of these things we find in the woods and the weeds. My guys and gals gotta get familiar with 'em."

"You teaching them to dodge these bullets?" Em waves the Desert Eagle—muzzle away from friendlies...

"More like: some idiot opens up on you, they waste the clip or's the gun got live rounds? The thing single action? Can you disarm 'em? What if he's got a hold-out? Quicker to use the gun in your holster sometimes."

Em gets it. "We're not supposed to disarm them. But you know that."

"I *do* know that."

Em gestures another *may I?* Hack nods once more.

The detective draws her Glock with the speed of *the man with no name* and fires five times. Each round hits perfect center mass. It's almost imperceptible but a little bitty tear runs down Em's cheek now. She looks a little off, then... Composure.

"Wow!" Hack says, meaning it. "If you ever want to do a guest lecture on anything ballistics, let me know."

Em puts on a mock tough guy, *"I'd rather let my gun do the talkin'"* She waves over the novelty firearms suggesting Hack give it a try too.

Without missing a beat he picks up a ten-gauge lever-action shotgun and *BOOM!* Blows what's left of Em's target to bits.

Em's amused.

"Effective," Hack acknowledges. He gets a little serious. "So, are you looking to transition into mercenary work, detective?"

"I thought I'd try asking you a few questions about what you've seen at the Reime residence. Anything that could help us..."

"But?" Hack asks, picking up on Em's hesitant tone.

"*But...* I don't imagine you discuss your clients' affairs as a matter of professionalism?"

"You got that right. However, Mr. Reime was quite clear that we were to help you in any way you needed and that included telling you everything we knew about Mr. Reime, warts and all. He said, and I quote, *the efficiency of any organization lives or dies depending on transparency.* I happen to agree."

"Interesting fellow," she says half-noncommittal. "What do you think about him?"

"He's scared."

Chapter 7

The Principal's Office

Another massive picket takes place outside an Alom fulfillment center. A local farmer has allowed picketers the use of his field adjacent Alom's compound. It's a carnival. It's nuts. But it's futile. You see, there are nearly as many robots inside the center as there are picketers outside. Products inside are sorted, selected, and moved by Roomba vacuums. Not literally—almost. Eight-inch-high orange pedestals on wheels pick up entire shelves of goods and move them in and out of the massive warehouse. A single one can move and sort more goods in a four-hour span of time than four human staffers can in an eight-hour shift. Staff went on strike and management just bought more vacuums. The picketers are on a fool's errand therefore. They have no leverage. Can't exactly call a robot a *scab* either. For this strike to work, literally all workers would have to be able to hold out for months and months. It's an *if you want one of us, you take all of* us scenario. Again, months and months.

The robots don't build and maintain themselves though...

Em inches to a stop at one of the approaches leading into the field. She's hardly there a minute when the back door of her car pops open and a picket sign is tossed onto the backseat. Then...

Gregory slides into the front seat and Em starts backing out of the approach.

"Looks like they're getting paid," kid says putting on his seat belt.

"You use the lines I gave you?"

"I *finessed* the lines you gave me. You actually used to be working class?"

"A cop's working class, ya butt."

"*Easy*... Not only did everyone I manage to press receive their first week's eighty percent, they all got a surprise two-hundred dollar picket stipend."

Em seems disappointed. "More pay than we ever got. It'll dry up."

Gregory cocks his head, looks at Em a little dubious. "What's this got to do with Park's murder?"

"Park's a victim of an injustice. Strikers are victims of an injustice. They're all caught up in the web of injustice. There's your connection."

"A little busy for grudges aren't you?"

"That's why you're doing the leg work junior." Em looks at the kid with a faux severity. "Who you been talking to you know about my grudges?"

"Called the switchboard. Asked about the nurse."

"I said ask *for* the nurse."

"Oops..." He smirks.

"Here." She holds out some cash.

"What's this?"

"CI pay. Minus the 'C'."

Kid shakes his head.

"What?" Em asks.

He takes the cash, looks at it in deliberation. "And here I thought I was an altruist."

"You are…"

Gregory goes from dubious to intrigued.

"…Because," Em explains, "the next time I'll ask you to do this for free and you'll do it all the same. There's always a reward, even if just peace of mind. *Take it when you've earned it, earn it even when you can't take it.*"

Gregory nods, pockets the cash. "This all you got?"

EM OPENS THE DOOR TO Leigh and Bomn. She hugs onto Leigh before the girl can even get through the threshold. She pulls away and squints at Bomn with mock scrutiny, then relents and gestures for him to bring it in for a hug too. Bomn obliges. The hug's surprisingly natural for a new boyfriend hugging the mother of his girlfriend. Downright strange for a police detective greeting an officer of seniority… Em breaks from Bomn and starts leading Leigh away.

"Go say hi to your father my dear. John and I will be right in."

"Oh, can't I stay for the bland procedural formalities?"

Leigh happily goes into the other room. Em focuses on her partner.

"Alright pro, I got a rule about shop talk on my day off, so let's get everything out up front, then it's Miller time."

"Nothing from me but some news on that Park address. It's commercial. It's called *Sun Pier Consulting*. Get this, mostly private investigations."

"Yeah, I know it. Called 'Sun Pier' cuz the guy that runs

it's named *Pearson*. Guy's a private investigator like Vlad the Impaler's a proctologist. Real seedy. We'll check him out tomorrow."

EM, BOB, LEIGH, AND JOHN BOMN are talking and laughing. Leigh's in the middle of a retelling of John's adventures in grade school education.

"*So you don't smooch?*" She makes playful kissy faces at John. "And Honest John just freezes like a deer in the headlights!"

They all laugh. John's getting hazed but he looks to be having a good time.

"Your mom froze like that the first time she laid eyes on me," Bob boasts.

"Cuz you were covered in puke!" Em corrects.

"Wasn't mine." Bob pantomimes waving off any responsibility. He leans in for an aside with John. "First residency..."

"Still waiting for the lab results on that one dear."

Raucous laughter. The levity's peaked.

There's nowhere for it to go but down. It's inevitable. It lessens. We know it's lessening because our diners are mock wiping their faces with napkins like there's even any food where it doesn't belong. There're some *ums* and *haws* too—the sounds polite company makes when a pleasantry is running its course. John even lets out one of those chuckles that indicate an appreciation of the humor if not the enjoyment of it. Like an old car chugging away a little despite the cutting of its engine. Lesser and lesser and lesser the levity goes... Until... Em turns to Leigh and tilts her head toward the living room. Leigh comprehends.

The girl gets up and hovers behind John. "Well, now it's time for *the talk*."

John looks to Em. Em comprehends.

"Not me. Him." Em points to Bob. Bob's giving a serious but warm look to the lad. The two ladies get up to leave.

"Gentle." Leigh says to her dad.

They go.

Bob, still serious, affects a pensive demeanor. Then...

"What do you think of curling, John?" He makes a curling sweeper sweeping motion.

"Um... My grandfather loves it. I watch it with him sometimes. Pretty good."

Bob's abrupt now, demanding. "Compare the sport of curling to any other game! Sport or otherwise!"

John thinks a second. "Chess."

BOOM! Bob smashes the table and guffaws. "You didn't say shuffleboard! Ya pass. You're good enough for my daughter!"

John chuckles—half bemused, half relieved.

Bob settles. "In all seriousness, I know ya enough—what little we spoke when Em took you under her wing for that *Detective's Apprenticeship* program. And now I know why we spoke so little when you were around here. You were focused on another Gray and it wasn't Em..."

John gets a little flushed.

"Ah, you're alright!" Bob insists. "Leigh vouches for ya and she's got a good head on her shoulders. Clincher is, working with Em, you gotta be a good soul because if you as much as stole a candy bar as a kid she'd have *felt* that guilt outta ya and would've told me all about it. Am I right?"

"Her ability to read people is really something else."

"I was talking about her blabbin', but alright." He smiles a smile intended to fade. Smile looks to have faded faster than Bob intended. The subject matter on which he's about to speak works the man's heart faster than his intentions work the will. There's no levity or irony now. He speaks in earnest. "You and Leigh are pretty serious or you wouldn't be here. I've gotten as close to learning to live with a cop who smashes through doors as I can. It'll never be close enough. Leigh hasn't even started to learn. Deal with this. Your wellbeing is her wellbeing now."

John nods.

"Alright!" Bob says, back to his unique brand of abrupt boisterousness. He gets up and gestures for John to rise as well. He talks as they walk. "I've been brewing my own lager old fashion style. This is the first batch where the cask didn't explode. You're gonna help me christen it!"

Bob looks over to Em all affectionate-like as they pass through the living room. Em smiles affectionately at him in return.

"Sounds great," says John.

Leigh looks to Bomn warmly but with a hint of a *hope it's going alright* in her expression. The two men exit. Mother turns to daughter.

"If he explodes that cask of beer all over your boy, I think it's safe to say he approves."

A pause.

A *BOOM!*

"I'll get some towels."

THE OFFICE SPACE OF SUN Pier looks like a principal's office. Desks in the back, waiting room up front, the two spaces separated by a tavern-like reception desk. Place appears empty though.

Em leans over the reception, getting a better look around. *Hello?*

Nothing.

Bomn notices a large bell on the counter. He gestures a *should I* to Em. Em shrugs a *dunno* back. Bomn picks up the bell and is about to give it a good ring when...

A bathroom door opens near the back of the place and a guy who must be the proprietor exits. He's wearing track pants and a t-shirt. He jogs on the spot.

"Ah shit, didn't hear ya," he shouts as his jog-on-the-spot becomes a jog-on-multiple-spots-linearly. He's slowly propelling himself toward the front desk, pitter by patter.

"Chester Pearson?" asks Bomn.

"That's right. Chester B. Pearson of *Sun Pier Consulting*. Clever name, I know." He moves through the swinging saloon door of the reception counter, past the detectives, and sits in a waiting area chair with some ankle weights in front of it.

"Caught me in the middle of a workout," he says, real jovial about things. He starts putting on the ankle weights. "Yeah, I know what you're thinking, *he's fat as shit*. Well, hence the workout. Go easy on me. Middle age ain't pretty."

"No arguments from me," Em says. "Pushing fifty." She pulls her badge wallet out of her breast pocket, holds it closer to Pearson. "Detectives Gray and Bomn. Talk a minute before the Ironman?"

"What about?" asks Pearson, a little cagey now.

"The Bertrand Park murder," says Bomn.

"Why do you want to talk about him?"

"His company travel records indicate he's been to this address three times the last few weeks," Em says.

"Thought he might be a client of yours," Bomn adds.

"I'm sorry, I can't discuss that."

"So, he *was* a client?" Em probes.

"I didn't say that. That's why I can't discuss that. So one way or the other, you'll have no way of knowing *that*."

"You don't want to help catch his killer?" asks Bomn.

"He's dead?" Pearson seems genuinely surprised.

"Not up on the news?"

"I don't think I'd miss if Charles Reime was murdered too."

"Now, isn't that interesting..." says Bomn. "I never mentioned Charles Reime. She never mentioned Charles Reime."

Pearson looks like he knows he messed up. Em notices.

"Listen, Mr. Pearson, you should tell us all you know now. Why bring warrants into what's been cordial so far?"

Pearson chuckles. "*And you don't want to get hung up on obstruction either...*"

Em gets dead serious. "If I'm gonna get you, I don't want you on anything as chicken shit as obstruction. Someone with your past? Think you'd be smart about keeping people like my partner and me as far away as possible."

"Boy, you guys sure don't play nice."

"Don't. Play."

"Alright alright," Pearson relents. "Bertie Park *was* a client. I had Charles Reime on my mind because I figured he must be your best suspect. See, that's who Park hired me to investigate. He wanted to know if Reime was up to anything at the company. Real suspicious."

"And, what did you find?" Bomn asks.

"Nothing."

"Nothing?" Em asks, seeking confirmation.

"A big fat pile of conspicuous nothing. Guy's clean. *Too*

clean. Even priests swipe cash from the collection plate, right?"

"I heard they do worse than that."

"You know what I mean. It's like the guy's been covering his tracks for a while now. Too goddamn clean."

"Maybe Reime's just that virtuous?"

"Oh come on. The biggest untouchable in the world buys it right after trying to take down the second. Don't gotta be a dick to know Reime's good for it."

"But you didn't feel any need to come forward with any of the information you'd gathered?"

"I ain't gonna risk crossing Charles Reime! He already knows about my investigation for crissakes."

"How do you know he knows?" Em asks.

"If you have access to Park-Mart travel records, Reime does too." Pearson looks at Em insistently. "Right? *Right?*"

Em exhales sharply, like maybe *she* messed up too.

"Don't tell anyone we told you this..." she says in a sympathetic tone. "But Reime put us on to you."

"Oh Christ! Oh Jesus!"

"Look," Em says, back to business. "You want to know what I think? I *don't* think Reime's 'good for it'. Either way, you want to protect yourself, help our investigation in any way you can. We catch the bad guys and Reime's involved, you're safe. We catch the bad guys and Reime's not involved, you're just as safe."

"Anything. Anything," Pearson insists.

Em gestures to Bomn half-encouragingly. "Detective?"

She moves out of Pearson's eyeline and leans on the front desk.

Bomn takes the lead. "You can start by giving us everything you have on Reime, but especially—"

CRASH! BING!

Pearson turns to the source of the clamor. His slow methodical scan around the room catches Em just having knocked the large brass bell off the counter. He brandishes an annoyed scowl for just an instant.

Em goes contrite. "Oh geez! I'm sorry. I was reaching for that pen and... I'm a clumsy ass sometimes. You two continue." Em bends down to retrieve the bell. She's behind the counter and out of sight. We hear her disembodied voice say in reminder, "Detective?"

AHEM! Bomn clears, "But especially anything you have on Reime in connection with Park. No matter how irrelevant you think it might be."

"You got it!" Pearson assures. "Everything! Let me talk to my associates and start getting copies of the documents. Re-corroborating any testimony... Tell you what, two days and I'll have it. Yours. Come by in two."

Em pops back up holding that bell, hand cupped inside to muffle any jingle as she puts it back in its spot. "Appreciate it. In the meantime, take all necessary precautions. And try not to worry yourself too much. Don't do anything rash."

"Done, done, and done! See, all us for-profits got an agreement: *business is business and all's fair in competing for clients, but when wellbeing's at issue, we band together.*" Pearson gets a proud look. "I've done security for I don't know how many dix when cheatin' husbands would come stalking around lookin' for the negatives. They owe me."

Em nods. She moves for the exit, Bomn follows.

DETECTIVES GET TO THE CAR. Bomn looks apprehensive again though in a different kinda way. The budding detective in him is starting to bloom.

"You're up to something."

"Yeah?" Em says, receptive to the sleuthing.

They both get in the car.

"Yeah," says Bomn, putting on his seat belt. "Telling him about Reime?"

Em grins. "Good, partner. That palooka's acting like he's scared to death but he doesn't jump at the clamor? Reime's scared. This guy's a ham. Let's see what comes of it."

Chapter 8

Information Technology

A set of *UPWU* records sits on Em's desk. Burgess has delivered what she promised, a weekly bundle of documents detailing all financial goings on at the *Yoo-Pee-Triple-Yoo*. Em is looking through the materials. Bomn is looking through Em.

"Major said to turn those in," he says.

"He already has his copy," she responds, flip.

"Detective..."

"H'archy Hoffa's sending them to me. Ain't it an obligation?"

"*Em...*"

"On my way to the Major's right now," she relents.

She grabs the stack of documents and heads down the hall. Like out of a cartoon, she turns down the corridor with a little sign that says 'Administration' but hangs a loopy half U-eey into the room opposite. Another officer exits that room with his own stack of documents. He's trying to walk and collate his photocopies at the same time.

Bohm's shaking his head in annoyance when...

Em pops her head back out the door.

"Don't worry partner. I made a promise. It's an *obligation.*"

A TECH WALKS EM AND Bomn through all surveillance video relevant to the Park case. They're viewing a recording of Park's walk through the grove he and his late wife frequented. They watch on a ninety-inch OLED screen surrounded by computer interfaces and controls. Screen is frozen on the Grove exit.

"Alright, Park goes in, doesn't come out. What happened in the interim? What are we missing?" Em asks.

"Could you have failed to index anyone?" Bomn says to the tech.

"If they're in frame," the tech says, "They're indexed to every discernible attribute."

"*Being Park's Killer* wouldn't happen to be one of those attributes would it?" Em asks, half sarcastic, half hoping.

Tech livens up like there's hope yet. "Interesting you should mention that. I've been writing an algorithm that identifies subtle behavioral and expressive traits universal among psychopaths, psychotics, and similar pathologies."

"Shit, run it then," Em demands.

The Tech goes to the controls. She futzes around a little, then... A picture of Em pops up on the screen.

"Here's somebody crazy enough to believe that algorithm bullshit."

Tech and Bomn laugh.

"Ha ha assholes. Now do *people in this room who shouldn't be fuckin' with a perimenopausal insomniac with a gun...*" Em gets back to serious. "We don't have the resources to ID all the people we'd have to." She pauses, thinking... Thinking... Starts monologuing under her breath,

"*WAMN* knows all of Brandon PD's blind spots too? Nah, whoever did this is a pro. Avoided every single camera." She glances around the viewing room as she's thinking out loud. She notices an envelope with 'DU' on it. "What's that?" she says, pointing.

Tech picks up the envelope making a *this?* gesture. "Conservationist group stuff. Motion sensor stills of duck boxes."

"Duck boxes?"

"Boxes built for ducks to nest in."

"You have a look?"

"Haven't had time," says the tech. "Have at it." She tosses the envelope to Em.

Em cracks into it and starts flipping through the photos. She stops. Flips back one photo, then to the next, then back again. "You got these in digital?"

Tech nods.

"Bring up 15-FG and 15-FH."

The OLED screen displays a curved panorama image of a pond. The image has been digitally straightened and appears warped on the video screen—think what the world would look like if you flattened a globe. The path that Mr. Park walked on curves down from the top/center edge of the image. You can just barely see a meter or two of the walkway dipping in from the top.

"Push in there," Em says.

Tech obliges.

"Look." It's someone only visible from the left bicep down. "That's Park's cane, clothes match too. Next." The tech moves to an image of another man in the same location, also only visible from the left bicep down. Em squints at the image. "Ok, who's this guy? Tip of Park's cane *there*, so this guy's right on Park's heels."

Bomn notices something. "What's that Em?"

"Where?"

"Guy's got something in his left hand."

In photo, we see that the left hand of the figure is mid-swing, moving backward as he strides. There's a discoloration near the wrist.

"Push in on the hand." Em says.

In photo, again, we see what looks like a gray/white discoloration and mass around the figure's wrist.

"That's not *in* his hand," Em realizes. "It's on it. It's a cast. Bomn?"

"Gotta be. Or some sort of medical brace."

"Bring back any PD surveillance indexed for *adult males, dark clothing, long sleeves...* I think that's all we can confirm."

Tech brings up some stills of people with these attributes. She flips through them. *Click.* No cast. *Click.* No cast. *Click.* No—

"Wait." Em's leaning in. "There it is. Play that."

In the video we see the man, hooded and unidentifiable, average height, cast on his left arm. He's walking with a limp into the Grove opposite the direction Mr. Park walks.

"Alright, better than nothing." Em speaks to the tech now, "Do me a favor, look for anything else with this guy."

Tech nods.

"I can tell Tesque about *limpy*," offers Bomn.

"Good. I'm going home. Gonna work out the logistics of checking every *WAMN* moron for fractures. From my tub." She pops a melatonin.

NEXT DAY. LEIGH AND EM sit at the kitchen island having just finished a late lunch. Em's holding her FatButt™

between her thumb and index finger. Leigh's trying to ignore this.

Em let's go of the device. "*Inconclusive.*" She angles the watch at Leigh. Watch says *ECG Inconclusive* and there's a digital representation of a human heart. "What do you think?"

"I think you're trying to diagnose a heart condition with a wristwatch."

"Are you from the past? This thing is state of the art, Ms. Luddite."

"There's literally a doctor in the other room who says your watch don't know *jack.*"

There's a knock at the door. We see Bomn in the door window. Leigh gets up to let him in.

Em calls after, "Yeah, but he ain't state of the art either."

Em's phone buzzes. She looks quick, talks quicker.

"Shit! Gotta meet my *CI* minus the *C.*" She talks at Bomn as she passes him going out the door. "You go pick up whatever Pearson's found for us. Maybe we'll get lucky and a big picture'll start coming together. I'll catch up with you..."

She bolts. Bomn notices the haste. Door slams. "That's the third time this week your mom's left me holding the bag."

Leigh reaches out and pulls him close. "Oh, is that what you call me?"

"It's a designer bag..."

She womps him one.

Chapter 9

The World Changes the Story, the Story Doesn't Change the World

It's a *WAMN protest*. Their word. It's at a Park-Mart store. Gregory moves about the masked demonstrators, all of whom are chanting identitarian slogans. He tries to blend in but looks simultaneously too civil and too young.

"I'm not recording you," says a frightened girl angling her phone at the activists. Email app is clearly visible on screen.

The young woman is surrounded by *WAMN* members pawing at her and grabbing for her phone. They want her to stop 'harassing' them and leave but are surrounding her and keeping her from going anywhere at the same time. Typical intimidation tactic. Gregory's standing just close enough to the struggling woman to know he's obligated to do something but it's fight, flight, or freeze for him and freeze is winning. He knows he has to intervene and he knows intervention constitutes *fight* on this equation, but his hardwiring sure doesn't. Instinct's a zombie lobotomized. He's locked in a state of fearful hesitation and hating himself for it. Then... *WAMN* thugs disperse as security approaches and the young woman bolts for the inside of the store. Gregory's relieved at the resolution if not still down on himself for his hesitation. He catches sight of something—brings greater relief through distraction, thankfully.

KID BURSTS INTO THE CAR and it pulls away from the storefront.

"Please. Please." he says, animated. "Throw me inna razor blades inna blender inna meat grinder before you throw me inna den of world-savers again."

"Not a fan of heroes?" Em asks.

"Ought to be a mental illness to believe you can save the world. Ought to be a crime to try."

"It ought."

"My dad used to say, *fix only the corners you can or leave well enough alone.* Don't let anyone ever accuse a h'archy of humility though."

Em smirks. "I'll inform my fellow *h'archies* of your dad's wisdom."

"You get a pass."

Em's touched... "Tell me about him."

Gregory doesn't hesitate, starts talking. Now Em's touched for real and for true.

"Met my mom shortly after he emigrated from Nigeria," he says, "she, Ukraine. At their ESL class. Marriage... Kids... Great provider... Better father... Died in a car accident coming home from a shift at the hospital... I loved the guy. Miss him every day." He says all this rapid fire.

"What are the chances, you split him in two you'd get your brother the provider and you the defender?"

"Pretty good," kid says getting back to the reason he's riding. "No casts, limps, injuries." He holds out an SD card.

"What's this?" Em asks.

"Copies of stills and video from *that*." He points back in the direction of the protest.

"I didn't ask for this," she warns.

"Couldn't help it. It's what I do."

"Jimmy Olsen?"

"That guy gets paid..."

She takes the SD card. "I appreciate it, but waving a camera around those guys is not a good idea."

"Nah."

"So sure?"

Gregory takes his phone out of his pocket and shows Em herself on the screen. He jostles his glasses a little and the video image shakes in perfect coincidence. Em comprehends.

"Won't take them long to spot those."

"I change the method. The bigger risk's those misguided souls catching on I'm not hiding an acid heart in sweet euphemism. Guy like me's their foil though. I get a minute more tolerance for that." He looks back again like they're following him. Never know...

"It's the critical mass of thug hangers-on you really need to worry about," Em warns. "The true believers are just talk."

"Talkers called a sweet old man a *fascist* for helping a high-schooler they pushed to the ground. They even know the meaning of their words?"

"They only care about the connotations," she assures.

"Connotations don't apply if the denotations don't."

"They don't believe in anything to denote."

"What the hell *do* they believe in, then?"

"Connotations."

"Come on..."

"Imagine this Gregory. Imagine they really—and I mean *really*—believe that just describing the world *some* way makes the world *that* way."

"Come on..."

"You *come on,* junior. I'm serious."

"Nobody really believes that. That's just what h'archies tell themselves when reality's too much to bear."

"*If there's something to believe, there are believers to believe it.* And, for these true believers, there's nothing to existence but the tales people tell of it. And I don't mean they think they need just spout a fiction long enough and everyone believes it. I mean they think themselves little gods on earth who need only utter *the word* and that makes it so. Like, *let there be light and there was light* type word. They don't get the world they want, they tell a story of the world they do. But anyone can tell a story, so they're in a constant struggle to ensure their story is *the* story. They tell it then stamp out anyone who says otherwise. They stamp out anyone who says otherwise because saying otherwise is to tell a different tale and that means a different world from the one they want.

"They resent the hell out of the people who rewrite their world. People like that old man who, with just a simple gesture, told a tale of their belligerence, hence defect. For that they utter into the void something like *that kindly old man is a baaaad kindly old man!* and that new story is all it takes to make a perfectly noble person bad people.

"There are awful feelings deep down inside for them, though, in all their resentment, so they describe themselves as *the good* in addition. Now, that may relieve them of their hatefulness on matters of the facts they think they're pulling out their asses, but it doesn't relieve them of those awful feelings. Those feelings are reality shoving itself down their throats and they can't dispense with that and that will be their undoing. But until they can no longer stand the dissonance of living in that insular little hole they've dug for themselves—to hide away from the clever contradiction of the realist and the passive contradiction of their damned senses—they'll go on."

She looks over to the kid. To her surprise he's listening. She hedges anyways... "Listen Gregory, I know it all sounds so silly, yet damned if that explanation doesn't account for how those fools can go around saying the patently absurd things they say. Like when they call some kindly old Good Samaritan a *fascist*."

"They profess the Good Samaritan's values..."

"They *profess* those values. The old man *lives* them. No matter the lengths they go in denying the reality of that old man's movements in the world, and theirs, his peaceful defiance stifles them in a way palpable. The world they deny's right back at their heels. Compounds the dissonance. Of course, if all you believe in are slogans, slogans are your only recourse. So it's back to spouting mean things about a nice man while spouting nice things about mean ivory tower extremists."

"That's delusion."

"*That's* what comes of being the type. The type who can't see out the window for his reflection in the pane. From being kept his whole life. Nobody's ever told these people *no*. Nobody's ever told them *otherwise*. So they get out into the big bad world and their general lack of ability necessitates nothing but *nos* and *that ain't sos*. They can't very well develop a thick skin and follow your dad's principles. They're the most self-absorbed people you'll ever meet. *They're so important they're going to save the world* kind of self-absorbed. However, if the whole world isn't something they can fix, then that's a limitation and a limitation is a flaw, and they won't admit flaws."

"They ever consider the world doesn't need fixing save for the parts they make worse?"

"Something perfect that isn't their doing? Doesn't exist for them. They want the *whole* world to save, and yet they couldn't save a tick from a dog. So they bury their heads in the sand of an existence where all there are are their stories, and their favorite story is the one where they save the world."

"Heavy theorizing for a cop, Em..."

Guess she has been psychologizing a lot lately, philosophizing even, like the front seat of her car's Plato's academy and she's corrupting the youth. Maybe it's time for the upshot, then she'll *leave well enough alone?* "Never stop being a realist Gregory. If you don't like the story of your corner of the world, change the world not the story."

BOMN'S FINALLY GETTING TO RING the bell at Pearson's front desk.

RING-A-DING-DING!

He finishes the summons and waits for the proprietor to emerge.

Waits and waits...

Bored, he leans onto and over the desk to get a better look around the place.

As he does, a figure moves through the front doorway of the office, entering quietly, methodically. Bomn's back remains turned to the figure as the figure's left-hand reaches out toward him. The hand gets just close enough to touch Bomn's shoulder when...

"*GEEZ!*" Bomn shouts, spinning. He catches sight of

Pearson, standing there looking at him, smiling in that sweaty tracksuit of his. "Scared the hell outta me Pearson!" Bomn reproaches.

"It's Chester... And sorry fella."

Pearson starts removing his track jacket. He pulls the left sleeve off first, revealing a pasty but toned forearm and bicep. He removes the rest of the coat. The wrist of Pearson's right arm has one of his light gray ankle weights wrapped around it. Bomn notices immediately.

Pearson notices Bomn noticing. "What? This thing?" He holds up the ankle weight and wobbles it on his wrist. "Fat fuckin' ankles. Keeps poppin' off my foot like the belts that inspired these walks kept poppin' off my gut!" Pearson walks over to the chair to take off the last lonely ankle weight. The asymmetry causes an undeniable limp.

Bomn looks furtively at the imbalance-in-stride.

Pearson sits, peeling apart the velcro. "Hope ya brought a wheelbarrow kid!" He bursts out of his seat. "The piles of documents I got for *you*." He moves off into the back of the shop and disappears behind a door.

Bomn immediately starts texting Em.

> Pearson susp...

Then...

DING!

Detective spins around. His eyes catch Pearson, barely, briefly. Guy's doubled back around front. He's raised his desk bell, poised to strike.

CRACK!

Bell smashes Bomn across the right cheek. Bomn goes down. Pearson immediately lowers himself onto the detective, pinning him down between his thick legs. He raises the bell again and smashes it into the back of Bomn's head. He's raising it a third time when...

EEEEEEEE!

A scream blurts from a passerby who can see everything through the large shop window. Pearson doesn't even look for the screamer. He lifts himself off Bomn, drops the bell, and runs for the back door.

Bomn's motionless. Blood everywhere.

Chapter 10

Neighborhood Watch

Em's car screeches to a halt in front of Pearson's office. She breaks out of it like she could care less about the EMS and cop vehicles in the vicinity— not to mention the procedure everywhere.

She motions for Gregory to stay in the car as she pushes toward the office with panic, concern, and determination fighting it out for what's left of any expression on her face. She's moving past the rear of an ambulance when...

"Detective..." says a voice, faint.

She turns. Relief. It's Bomn sitting on the rear of the ambulance, holding an ice pack to the back of his head. He's trying to look into the penlight of an EMS worker but is staring more into the mid-afternoon sun than anything else.

Em holds her coat up, spanned-out over her head like she's scaring off a bear. She successfully blocks out the sun for the EMS worker.

"Thanks," the worker says.

Em turns to Bomn, "How are you?" She turns to the EMS worker before Bomn can answer. "How is he?"

"Got my bell rung," Bomn says, labored but jokey. Em's

only concerned, unreceptive to the pun. Bomn realizes this. "Oh right," he labors "You just got here."

EMS finishes the once-over. "He's concussed." She says to Em. "Could be a minor fracture, but I doubt it. He was lucky the weapon had the curvature it did." She points to the bell in an evidence bag. Em gets the pun. EMS moves back to the front of the ambulance, out of sight.

"I'm sorry," Bomn offers Em weakly.

"Why?" she asks.

"Got me and got away."

"You ID'd him didn't ya?" Em holds up her phone.

Pearson suspect. Cast was ankle weight.

Dont confrot. Backup coming

"Yeah." says Bomn.

"So ya did great."

"Yeah?"

"Yeah. And now you're gonna go for a fun ride in a *am-u-lance* and sleep in your very own hospital bed."

Bomn's face lowers. His mood changes. "I'm scared."

"It's just for observation. You'll be fine."

"I'm scared of Leigh."

"You should be scared of me!"

"I'm scared for Leigh. I'm scared *of... For* how she'll take this."

Em's a little taken aback at this. It's more significant a statement than us civilians will ever understand. She strokes Bomn's cheek and nods in understanding.

GREGORY'S PLACE—THERE'S A BIT of a debrief going on. The kid and Em chat.

"We got lucky today," she says. "This could have been so much worse."

The two just sit a minute, stewing in the catharsis brought about by Em's platitude. Then...

"Well," Em sighs. "Gotta go." But she isn't moving just yet. "Been ordered back to supervise Reime's security detail." Detail's unnecessary but department-approved due Pearson's potential targeting of Reime. It's all formality and Em knows it. It's all formality and Em doesn't care about it either. Make no mistake, she wants Pearson on a hook, but that palooka ain't coming to the castle and Em's got more important men in her life to worry about. She's gotta go but isn't moving just yet. She looks at the kid with an expression of understanding and a feeling of neglect in her gut— neglect all over the place. "I know what you saw in that crowd's got you thinking about what you did and didn't do," she says to Gregory.

Kid raises an eyebrow. "You can tell that, huh?"

"I know how you feel. Hell, I'm feeling the same. Shoulda been backing the kid up. Should have been there to stop Pearson. Feeling it to... So, the least I can do is not neglect you in addition." She smiles a smile of *please forgive* and continues. "Unlike my negligent ass, you got nothing to worry about. Make no mistake, this neighborhood here, the state of it, means you have nothing to ever be ashamed of." She baps the kid on the shoulder. She looks at him, then all around, to herself in the mirror, back at him, real wistful. "I never met your dad," she says, then nods at herself like *I've got it though*. "But I know he'd be proud. Your brother too."

It's nothing but silent comprehension in the kid as... His little brother Pet pops into the front passenger-side window. He's there to greet the two. Gregory smiles warmly at his little brother, Em too. Pet's now leaning on the car, a part of the debrief.

Down the block, about four houses back, a late-sixties-era muscle car sits, idling. It's parked on the opposite side of the block as Em's car though facing the same direction. Kinda brazen, as per this guy's norm. One of the many exploiters of the down and dependent—call him *Carpetbagger Thug*—sits in the passenger seat. He's flipping through some photographs while a driver and a backseat passenger wait patiently. We can only see the photos at a distance, though it's clear they're of Thug engaged in some sort of criminal activity. Thug looks up and over to Em's car. He points to it. Driver and passenger nod.

WE'RE BACK AT THE REIME mansion. Em is discussing things with another detective and two uniformed police. Charlie and Aylynn are talking with Hack, likely about similar subject matters. The Reimes both look sufficiently concerned, a little distraught. Em finishes with the police and moves to talk with them.

"We appreciate your cooperation you two. This will be over as soon as we apprehend Pearson. Then we'll be out of your family's hair."

Charlie sounds at a loss. "He hired a private investigator. Why? Why do you think he did it detective?"

"I'm not sure," Em relents. "Pearson said it was a general suspicion, but we obviously can't trust his word."

"No, not that." Charlie smiles a little in affection. "Bertie had it in his head I was trying to move Park-Mart exclusively online, behind his back. I'm sure that's why he hired Pearson." He gets earnest. "I mean, why did Pearson kill Bertie?"

Em hesitates for a second, then... "Pearson was not a good man. From all I've heard, Mr. Park was. I think this was an unfortunate coming together of two people. One trusting, the other more than willing to take advantage of someone trusting. I'm sorry, Mr. Reime."

Aylynn starts to cry. Charlie comforts her.

Em's phone rings. "Excuse me," she says stepping toward the hallway.

SHE PUTS THE PHONE TO her ear as she exits Reime's office.

"Eminence Gr—" Voice on the other end shifts Em's demeanor on a dime. It's a panicked grief in the detective, but she tries to maintain a sense of calm, stoicism even. "I'm sorry... Mrs. Hrominchuk... I can barely understand. Where are you? Please tell me where you are."

EM JOGS TOWARD INTENSIVE CARE. She'd run faster but she doesn't want to risk disrupting hospital proceedings. She also needs to keep her bearings. She gets closer and she's able to make out Gregory's mom and sister sitting in the intensive care waiting area. They're holding onto each other, distraught.

Her phone's ringing now. She ignores it.

Mrs. Hrominchuk sees Em and rises. She moves toward Em.

"Mrs. Roman—"

Mrs. Hrominchuk starts punching—really, flailing—at Em. "This is your fault! He's not waking up! He's not waking up!"

Her flailing breaks down into a holding—then embracing—of Em.

"What happened?" Em says, trying to hide the pleading in her voice.

"They beat him. They beat him. They torture him!" the mother wails.

A nurse rushes over.

"Excuse me ma'am? I'm sorry, I can help with your questions, but you can't be... The noise..."

Em nods. She walks Mrs. Hrominchuk back to her daughter, still in the embrace. Em's phone rings again. She sits Mrs. Hrominchuk down and then turns off the ringer.

"What happened?" Em asks looking up at the nurse, holding just Mrs. Hrominchuk's hand now.

"The Idris boy?"

"Yes!" she says, aggravated and curt. "Sorry."

The nurse understands. "He's in an induced coma. He was very badly beaten. It doesn't look good, but he's young and he's strong."

"I know."

EVERYTHING'S INVERTED NOW. EM'S MOVING slowly—getting slower—toward the hospital bed. She needs to move faster but she can't. It's not a *finding her bearings* thing this time, she just can't. She inches closer and closer though. Her eyes well up in a blur: impairment sustaining an ignorance of things, of the boy's state. This allows her the crossing of Zeno's gap.

She blinks out the tears. She finally looks...

It's Pet. Everything about his appearance is consistent with his mom and the nurse's descriptions. It's horrible.

"They thought he was me," says a voice behind Em.

She turns to see Gregory standing in front the partially closed curtain of Pet's bed. She looks relieved. She can't help looking that way. She latches onto him. Tears stream from her eyes. He hugs her back in a way that indicates he cares but has a mission that doesn't permit sentimentality.

Em pulls back and starts to collect herself. Gregory continues.

"Thought he was the one taking the pictures. Went into convulsions sayin', *kept callin' me rat big brother, kept callin' me rat.* Pieces of shit called my brother a *rat* like they want us to know they're from a million miles away, from goddamn TV, here to take what we built."

"I'm going to do everything I can—"

"They tortured him on our front lawn. In front of everyone. Nobody did a thing to help. My mom and sister found him coming home."

"I'm going to do everything I can, but you're out of this. No more helping me. No more stalking around playing photojournalist." Gregory looks at her with nothing but fire. Em comprehends. "I'll bust you the second you step out of bounds and your mom'll put the cuffs on. You know this right?"

"I know the criminal code better than you do. You know this right?"

"Yeah."

He's gone.

EM DRIVES. SHE'S TAKING HER pulse again, but she can't risk popping that melatonin yet. She's amped up and feeding off it. She's turned her phone back on and is in the middle of a call.

"What do you mean you can't put a detail on the house? The kid was beaten within an inch of his life— *FUCK!*"

Cop lights flash behind her. She pulls over.

"Fuck bye!"

She looks like she doesn't know why she said those words. She's tired. She turns off her phone again. Grabs her badge and exits the car trying to intercept the officer already exiting his vehicle.

"Real busy, guys," she says, badge waving.

Traffic officer stops, hands on belt, "That's why we've pulled you over Detective. We have orders to escort you back to the Reime estate."

"You fucking kidding me?"

"It's direct from The Major."

"And if I refuse?"

"Then we bring you to The Major."

"Oh that's real goddamn efficient. What, we're all heading over to his house in the middle of the night? Pajama Party? Gonna braid each other's hair?"

"We take you to The Major's office... *After*..." Cop flicks his handcuffs. Em comprehends.

"Fine. Let's go."

She gets back into her car. She turns her phone back on. It's already ringing. It's *Police Squad*. She ignores it one last time and starts dialing someone worth talking to.

That *someone* answers.

"Think you can do me a favor?" she asks.

THE WHOLE THREE BLOCKS ARE a mishmash of older brownstone and tenement houses imposed upon by large ten-story complexes randomly plopped down wherever enough vacant lots had emerged. It's a real maze inside but the residents have figured it out.

Carpetbagger Thug's car is tooling down the block, slow, staying in the parking lane next the curb. It makes a right without a signal and disappears around the corner. Seconds after it does, a figure emerges from between the parallel stairwells of some tenements. It's Gregory, stalking Thug. He moves briskly down the block, hugging the edges of the buildings as he approaches the same corner. He hesitates. Looks to be listening for something. He hears the unmistakable gurgle of the muscle car moving away. He rounds the corner.

BANG!

Kid's clobbered and knocked into the side of a bus-stop shelter. He crumbles down the shelter wall as Thug and his backseat henchman emerge from between two stairwells. Turns out they were playing the same game as Gregory. Thug watches Gregory struggling for a second, then...

"Well shit. It was *you* after all." Thug laughs. "Look at the real Laura Mars here," he says to his goons. "Went from taking pretty pictures to witnessing a serial killing. His."

Thug and goons move in as Gregory struggles to pull something out of the front pocket of his hoodie. They're wary at first, back off a little. Object emerges. Gregory's pulled that old-timey camera of his. Thugs recognize the object and erupt in mocking laughter. Then...

Gregory let's fly with the rapid-fire setting on the camera, flash and all. *CHIT! CHIT! CHIT! CHIT! CHIT!* The goons are blinded. They flail surreally due to the strobe effect. Gregory turns, is about to run, but holds up. He spins back and capitalizes on the blindness. He hoofs his brother's assailant right in the scrotum. *BOOM!* Shoves him into the bus stop.

Now he bolts, hanging a sharp left into a vacant lot and through it, coming to a narrow parking lot that runs perpendicular. He stops to survey the environment but hears his attackers' voices faint behind.

Looks Left... Right... Left...

There's another vacant lot leading back into the street to his left. He runs for it in a diagonal across the car park.

He comes ripping around the corner and into the lot's opening. He gets his bearings, braces to move forward when... Face contorts in despair. There's not just a large chain-link fence on the other end, but one that's top is lined with razor-wire. He moves to the fence searching for any opening. None. He smashes the mesh in frustration.

"We for sure hafta kill ya now."

The kid turns to see the goons at the open end of the lot. They're approaching slowly.

"Don't even care where the rest of your portfolio is. Shit, I can just move to another neighborhood, another town. Junkies everywhere itchin' for my *rent checks*." Thug pulls a large folding serrated pruning saw out of his waistband. Not so intimidating a weapon, one that's said to *fold* and be meant to *prune*. Sounds like something out of grandpa's work shed. In reality, the thing looks like a hooked machete with teeth. Thug folds out the blade, seems to be enjoying an intimate, lusty, camaraderie with the tool—real fetish. He bears teeth at Gregory and starts gloating about the boy's pending demise. "Now, we about to be goin', but before we do..." He waves the rusty scythe. He chuckles. The two henchmen pull guns and fix them on Gregory as Thug moves in.

Kid's still. He's his usual stoic though that stoicism only hides the fact he's defeated as hell. Thugs are getting closer. Maybe the kid's about to break but we'll never know because... A door in the brick wall to his right opens and all that *ruled!* about action movies back when action movies *ruled!* walks out.

Hack moves between Gregory and the goons.

He's calm.

He's calm but what's that matter any? An immovable object's calm to something coming at it at a thousand miles an hour. Doesn't mean the *comer* coming too fast isn't going to shit his pants through his ears at the sight. If there's time...

"Ah... H—ha..." chuckles Thug, voice faltering. "You're not from around here."

"Neither are you," Hack reminds. "And we're all going home. The easy way..."

Goons wait for the rest.

Silence.

"No *hard way*?" Thug musters.

"My ripping your head off sound like a task?" Hack's eyes narrow. He peers at the goons, sizing them up. "There's no *hard way* with you."

Goons scoff. Thug grimaces. All move in. Hack's arms open wide and low.

WE'RE WIDE-ANGLE LOOKING DOWN the street, vanishing point style. The sidewalk is at our center-left. The brownstone to the left of the vacant lot blocks our view of what's happening in that lot. For a split second, for all we know, it's just a quiet wet film noir street sleeping in the night. But...

BANG! BANG!

Some gunshots are heard and we can see muzzle flashes coming through the chain-link fence of the lot. There're some sounds of tussling, then silence again.

Then...

Carpetbagger Thug flies out of the vacant lot, upside down, enveloped in the chain-link fence he was tossed through and's now dragging along with him in midair. He lands in a trash heap next to the curb, a mess of wire and flesh. His henchmen run out after him, scattering away in different directions. Hack walks out after all this and stops. He analyzes the groaning Thug, legs wiggling in the razor wire. Thug's toast.

Gregory walks out now and stands beside Hack, dwarfed by the agent.

THE TWO SIT ON THE kid's porch, Hack on the phone with Em. The agent seems as familiar in the domesticity as Gregory. Similar life to get back to, perhaps? He's scanning around the neighborhood as he speaks. Scan stops on three of his agents standing by an agency vehicle parked out front.

"Three of my best will watch the neighborhood. Until."

"Until?" Em asks.

"Neighborhood either joins Gregory and we're redundant, or, they don't and we're redundant. My men become a permanent fixture, we've failed." He looks to Gregory. "Bet on the former. Until then, no one will ever know we're here."

Hack ends the call. He baps the kid on the shoulder and smiles at him. Smile turns to an expression of realization. Gregory's curious.

"Almost forgot." Hack reaches into his coat pocket. "You dropped this." He hands Gregory the old-timey camera.

Kid takes it. "Thanks."

"Where do you even get film for that thing?"

"Don't. It's empty."

"Saved ya tonight." Hack notices that Gregory's moving his thumb over a label maker label on the camera, caressing it nearly. The label's scuffed. Its lettering is no longer embossed but worn flush and flat to the tape's surface. What it says is,

Dennis Idris

Another look of realization on Hack's face.

Then...

"Keep t' walkin' boy or so help me..." says a voice down the street.

"Alright alright old man! Damn!" says another from the same location.

Hack and Gregory step off the porch looking toward a small group of neighborhood residents led by *Old Man Benny,* moving Thug's two henchmen toward Hack's agents. None are armed and the henchmen are not restrained, but they are detained.

"We would like to make a citizen's arrest," Benny requests of Hack.

"I will notify relevant law enforcement," Hack obliges.

Benny looks to the kid. "I'm sorry Gregory. We're sorry."

Gregory nods.

Chapter 11

You May Have Already Won

W e're back at the Reime mansion. It's been a couple days. Pearson's still on the lam but nowhere near dumb enough to target Reime. Nowhere near dumb enough to warrant the ongoing security detail. Nevertheless, the detail persists.

Em sits talking with Sydney and Aylynn in Charlie's office. Things are real cordial. Interestingly, Sydney has come around to Em and is smiling and laughing a good share of the time. Em must have worked some sort of magic or Mrs. Reime was right all along about her daughter's nature.

Mr. Reime is opening his mail by the fire. "Don't let anyone ever tell you money will stop Publisher's Clearing House from trying to convince you you need more." He throws some flyers and a *You May Have Already Won* letter into the flames.

KNOCK! KNOCK!

Em goes to the door as Reime flips to a plain pre-paid envelope with no return address. His appearance turns a little cagey. He opens the envelope and finds a small note inside. It reads,

11237824?
41 43'57'NICE 49 56'49'WORK

Em opens the door to Hack. There's a slight, near imperceptible flash of light as he moves over the threshold. Em smiles both in recognition and appreciation at the big merc as Reime burns the note and the rest of the junk mail.

He rises and excuses himself. "I think I'm going to get some air. Feeling a little cabin-fevery."

"I can send someone with you," Hack offers.

"Nah. It's the constant companionship that's the cause of said cabin fever." Reime chuckles.

He leaves the office.

IT'S JUST EM, SYDNEY, AND Hack. Aylynn has gone off to bed. Hack stands looking out the window as Em and Sydney play Uno and converse.

"I wouldn't stress about Leigh," Sydney assures. "If she didn't grow up in the ivory tower, she won't stay in the ivory tower. It's people like me you've got to worry about."

"Oh we do, my dear. We *all* do." Em smirks.

Syd rolls her eyes near all the way around.

"She's just always been so prudent and sensible," Em continues. "I'd hate to see that change."

"Well, if by sensible you mean keeping a careful critical eye, she should have gotten a philosophy degree like me."

"You heard me say she's prudent too, right?" Em says this deadpan.

Sydney laughs. "Wow! Walked right into it again! *Touché*."

SQUAWK! Hack's radio goes off.

"*Prom king*'s left the *dance*," says one of his agents. "Need confirmation on *chaperone*."

Em rises reflexively and starts scanning the room.

"What do you mean he's left?" Hack says into the radio.

"Five minutes ago. Said you were following."

Em's still scanning.

"What's happening Gabe?" Sydney asks, concern in her voice.

"Your dad's left the grounds," Hack says matter-of-factly. He softens. "Sure it's nothing, Syd. You know how he obsesses. Probably got it in his head he needed something at the office."

Em's ice. Still scanning. Then...

"The mail," she says. "He was going through the mail. Said it was junk mail but it wasn't *all* junk mail?"

Hack's trying to follow the stream of consciousness. "Em?"

"*Shit shit shit. Come on...*" the detective says, drumming her fingers on her stomach. "That flash!" She goes to the door, looks back at Hack. "There was a flash when I let you in. He left seconds after!" She moves to where Reime was sorting his mail. "He took a picture of something here, burned it. Left. *Maybe*... We gotta check those photos."

"He took his phone with him," Hack offers.

"But he's signed up for a cloud service he doesn't even know he has," Sydney rescues. She's already logging into her dad's desktop. She brings up the photos app. "Makes billion-dollar deals for breakfast," she says in hush, "can't use a computer to order lunch."

The three huddle around the computer as the last photo pops up. It's those arcane numbers.

"*Coordinates*." Hack says, already punching them into the routing app on his phone.

Sydney looks at the photo in concern. "What does that number mean? Em?"

"It's something important enough to get your dad's attention Syd. Other than that, I don't know, but we'll get to him and figure this out." She pats Sydney on the shoulder. Syd gestures some appreciation-carried-in-shudder. Em and Hack move for the door.

THE COORDINATES HAVE LED THE two to a plot of land just off the highway. They've parked up the gravel road and are moving toward a mobile home that sits on the property. Both have their side arms drawn.

As they get within a dozen yards of the trailer, they see all lights are off. Closer now, they see a car parked around back of the structure.

Hack points to it. "Charles'," he whispers.

The two investigators separate, moving in opposite directions around the trailer, popping up and peeking through each window as they go, then dropping back into the darkness. They meet around the other side.

"Too dark," Em relents.

Hack nods.

They each move to a different door of two on the front facade of the trailer.

THEY ENTER AT THE SAME time and get low behind objects in the virtual dark. Some illumination from the yard-light enters the windows. Gives the slightest of form to the interior of the mobile home. There's no sound or movement discernible.

Em reaches for a light switch above her. She flicks it. Nothing.

"No power," she says in Hack's direction.

"Kerosine," Hack notices.

"Smell it too. Real strong here."

"Got it."

Em turns on her mag light. Holds it in the direction of the kerosine smell. There's a broken lantern on the floor next to a dinner table. Em moves the flashlight up along the table. A body is draped over it as though it fell forward from a standing position. She recognizes the tracksuit.

"Pearson. Not moving."

She shuffles toward Pearson, low, as Hack turns on his own flashlight. He shines it around the living room area in which he hunkers. His beam reveals a second body, keeled over in an easy chair in the corner.

"Another." He rushes to it. "Oh god..."

Em enters the front of the living room. "Clear on my end."

She gets to the body Hack's discovered. The body holds a small pistol in right hand. Em's already got a glove on. She carefully lifts the head of the body, obviously a corpse. It's Reime.

"Oh god..."

A GENERATOR BUZZES AWAY POWERING large flood lights. They light up the plot like a stadium. EMS crews are packing it in—never any need for their services anyway—

and Techs are just getting started. Tesque is on the scene talking to Em and Hack.

"Prelims?"

"Looks..." Em says. "And I mean *looks* like Pearson lured Reime here. Either to kill him or it escalated to that. Pearson put two in Reime as Reime stood at the entrance of the living room but Reime pulled a pistol. Must have caught Pearson by surprise cuz Pearson only got the two shots off. Reime then emptied the whole clip at Pearson, hitting him five out of eight. After that Reime collapsed and crawled—miraculously considering Pearson's shot pattern—to the chair."

Tesque surveys in disgust. Shakes his head at what's coming at about a hundred yards out. The Major's arriving —groggy, angry, and in all but his silk pajamas. "How'd it get to this Gray?"

"I fucked up."

Chapter 12

-5

We're back in the detective's bullpen. Em's flipping through some photos. Some days must have passed because Bomn is back to work too, sitting across from her as professional as ever. Em continues flipping. She's looking at a picture of Gregory's neighborhood watch in action.

Flip...

Another picture of Gregory's neighborhood watch in-group, smiling, Gregory at the center.

Flip...

A picture of Gregory's family, Pet at the center, smiling from his hospital bed, surrounded by his family. A post-it attached to the photo says 'Thanks'.

Em tears up a little. Then...

"Eminence Gray?" A courier is wandering around the bullpen. "Eminence—"

"*Me.*" Em waves him over, wiping at her eyes.

Courier beelines to her. "For you." He hands her a small box. Looks like an engagement ring-holder-sized box.

She tears the wrapping off, opens the small paper

container, and pulls out a key. There's the tiniest of etchings on it that Em can barely read. She can't read it in that way where: if it's close enough it crosses her eyes and if it doesn't cross her eyes it's too blurry. She can't make it out for the life of her hyperopia.

She's up, moving swiftly toward her superior's office.

EM SWING'S THE DOOR OPEN. Dickie looks up.

"Yeah?" the sergeant says.

"Your eyes goin'?" she asks.

"I'm only three years older than you, Gray—"

"So's Bob. Can't see for shit."

Tesque looks at her. She looks back, not making a move. He squints at her.

She smiles at the tell. "Gimme those glasses." She moves to his desk, hand outstretched.

Tesque shakes his head in resignation, hands 'em over. "What you up to?"

"I'll tell you when I know myself." She holds the glasses up to the key like a magnifying glass. She can finally make out the message,

Union St.

204

She looks at the key barely a second before getting it. Looks disgusted with herself in the process. Get's something else. She tosses the reading glasses back to Dickie like they're burning her hands.

"Christ, I'm getting old."

.   .   .

WE'RE IN A STORAGE LOCKER bay at Union Station. Em pulls a legal-sized envelope out of a locker numbered '204'. She tears the top off it. Examines what's inside. It's just a letter. The letter reads:

> I, Chester Pearson, killed Bertrand Park. He hired me to investigate Charles Reime for any impropriety involving his role at Park-Mart Inc. Over the course of my investigation, I uncovered incontrovertible proof of Reime subsidizing various militant protest groups to cause breaches of the peace at Park-Mart centers, driving off customers, thereby justifying a shift toward online exclusive shipping and distribution (a shift Mr. Park was opposed to). I presented this information to Mr. Park on Tuesday, October 15th.

"I killed Bertrand Park..." Em whispers as she reads on.

> Shortly after, on Saturday, October 19th, Reime approached me about my investigation (I assume Mr. Park confronted Mr. Reime about the impropriety and the latter managed to ascertain my role in its discovery). Reime offered me $20,000 to destroy all evidence of the impropriety. I agreed. Reime offered me $80,000 to kill Mr. Park. I also agreed. In addition, I demanded $12,378.24 (expenses plus my standard fee).

"One-hundred and twelve-thousand three-hundred and

seventy-eight dollars and twenty-four cents. All told." Charlie Reime's note flashes before Em's mind's eye:

$$1\,1237824?$$
$$41\ 43'57'\text{NICE}\ 49\ 56'49'\text{WORK}$$

I'm not writing this to clear my conscience. This is my insurance policy. In the event that anything happens to me, I have arranged to have this letter of confession, implicating one Charles Reime of felony murder, released to the relevant authorities. Unfortunately, I have destroyed all evidence of the payoffs, in clear view of Mr. Reime, as per our arrangement. That said, expect another key to be delivered that will lead to evidence of Reime's solicitation of murder. I will be notifying Mr. Reime of this letter and the conditions for its release upon receipt of payment for our second arrangement. Again, for insurance purposes.

BACK IN THE BULLPEN. EM'S reading the note to Tesque and Bomn.

"*...He hired me to...*"

"Stop." Tesque insists. "Hear this lump in my throat Em? That's not me getting emotional." He cups the part of his throat he's referring to. "What you hear are my balls. I paid one of the pros in holding fifty bucks to kick 'em up there so The Major couldn't find 'em and bust 'em off! He's on his way here now so give me the *TLDR* before he buries this thing."

"Well, if you'd stop telling us about your sex life..." Em whispers this more than loud enough for Bomn to hear and snortle. Tesque hears too.

"Em!"

Business now: "Pearson, the PI, caught Reime paying *WAMN* to protest at Park-Mart to drive customers away from their physical stores. This was done to motivate a transition to online-only sales. A move Park was opposed to. Pearson presented the evidence to Park. Park presented it to Reime. Reime put two and two together, ran the investigation back to Pearson and offered him a hundred grand to destroy any evidence and kill Park."

"You buy it?"

"Not a cha—"

The Major and his bureaucrat barge into the office.

"Is that it?" The Major demands. "Is that the note?" He makes a few attempts at grabbing it but Em keeps flipping it back and out of his reach with each attempt. This goes on for *waaay* too long until Em decides to just let The Major have it. He rips the note out of her hand.

Bureaucrat gestures to Major. Major hops to it.

"Where and how did you get this, Detective Gray?"

"It's a standard sleazeball insurance policy," Em says. "Blackmail any co-conspirators into leaving you alone by threatening to release incriminating evidence to the relevant authorities should you meet some untimely fate. Pearson met some untimely fate. I'm the relevant authority."

"The testimony of some scummy hitman isn't exactly incriminating evidence," Tesque assures the Major.

"Surely there's more to incriminate this Pearson?" Major responds.

Em rips the letter back from the Major. Major gasps. Em recites. "*Unfortunately, I have destroyed all evidence of the pay-offs, in clear view of Mr. Reime, as per our arrangement.*"

Bureaucrat gestures to Major again, Major hops to it again, taking back the note.

"How many copies of this?"

THE MAJOR IS BRIEFING WHAT looks like the whole department on a heavily redacted version of Pearson's note. The note's projected onto a huge screen behind him and we can just make out that all statements incriminating Charlie Reime are blacked out.

The Major is pointing at the projection. "We clearly see that Pearson confesses to Park's murder," he says. "Further investigation is forthcoming but the facts of the matter are, in separate instances, Pearson assaulted a police officer and was found at the scene of Reime's murder, murder weapon on his person. Additionally, Pearson's is too consistent an account of the Park murder scenario, right down to the exploitation of *WAMN* demonstrators, to be a likely falsification."

Em leans over to Bomn like she's going to whisper, but says loud enough for everyone to hear, "*I wonder what's under all that black ink?*"

The Major flusters a little. He tries to *AHEM!* his way back to composure. "*AHEM!* Now, some of you may have heard that this note implicates Charles Reime as Pearson's co-conspirator. Well, for the sake of the Reime family, we are asking that all involved refrain from spreading any rumors about Mr. Reime's complicity, at least until more can be ascertained."

Em, Bomn, and Tesque look disgusted.

EM, BOMN, AND TESQUE WALK back to their respective desks.

"What are the chances the Major's office intercepts that second key?" Tesque asks.

"Note's bullshit," Em assures. "There's no key."

"Detective!"

The Major happened to be in earshot. He heard everything Em just said. He's pointing at Tesque's office.

"In here now!" he barks at her.

THE MAJOR SLAMS THE OFFICE door as Em enters, leaving Tesque locked out. "*That note* is all but proof that Reime's cooperation *was* misdirection. Mr. Helpful put you onto his partner in crime to take the heat off himself and you bloody fell for it!"

"Reime didn't feel—"

"You're not a goddamn mind reader Gray! Your gut failed you this time. Reime manipulated you."

"Don't know why he even bothered considering you guys were just gonna sweep his involvement under the rug..."

"Detective!" shouts The Major.

"That note's bullshit and if you let my brain catch up to my gut, I'll tell you why."

"I'll tell you what's *bullshit* detective. Two people are dead in addition to Park because instead of digging into Pearson's connection to Reime, you've spent the last three weeks trying to nail Nina Burgess on some nose-blind-hound of a misappropriation charge. As soon as I have proof you've been using department resources to investigate Burgess, you'll be on permanent suspension and up on charges!"

Em's fed up. "I'll save you the trouble of failing to close yet another of your cases, Major. I *have* been looking into Burgess. She's dirty. She's stealing that strike fund out from under those workers and I'm provin' it."

"You're fired is what you are!"

"Not even close."

"You've got some nerve."

Em opens the office door and gestures to Tesque. "Detective! In here now! *Please.*"

Tesque shakes his head in frustration. He walks toward the office staring daggers at Em.

Em beams at her sergeant—despite his dagger-eyes. "Could you explain to The Major the *Negative Fifth Law?*"

Tesque looks at Em with a *really?* look.

"What's she talking about Sergeant?" The Major demands.

Tesque breathes deep. Exhales. Shakes his head at Em and begins. "Alright... It's arcane, seldom invoked legislation: *any citizen attempting to exonerate his or herself of a crime...* known to be committed or not... *through formal legal channels, will be granted that privilege by...* and only by... *the investigative officer first approached.* The law was only ever used to dupe persons of interest into granting police full permission to investigate them using any departmental resources available. Since only a *suspect* could be cleared in a case, people seeking exoneration immediately defaulted themselves to *suspect* status. This meant police could treat them as such. Find some dummy you think is dirty but don't have enough on to start a formal investigation, let him know his exoneration is his for the asking. All he needs to do is ask and *BOOM!* suspect status. Assumed perp's just opened an investigation on himself. It's sleazy as all hell. We tend to not mention the negative fifth for this reason."

"I'm lost here detective. What's the upshot to all this?"

"Burgess provided Em with financial records toward the express purpose of Em clearing her. Not only is Em permitted to investigate Burgess, legally speaking, she's obligated to."

Em points to her -5 button. Tesque comprehends. The Major fumes.

"W—well... We'll see about that," Major says. "Either way, I want her off the Park case as of this instant!" He gets in Tesque's face now. "You better get a handle on your detectives!" The Major storms off.

Em shrugs at Tesque. Tesque looks like toast.

"He found 'em..." she says.

"Huh?"

She cups her throat. "Your fifty-dollar friends."

Chapter 13

Give up the Ghost

Em's watching the Diane Saint discussion for clues as to what Burgess is up to. She's also flipping through the records Burgess provided. She has everything spread out in front of her in no particular order as she moves randomly from her files to the recording. Files to recording... Files to recording... She can't seem to find what she's searching for. She flops her head back over the top of her chair and closes her eyes.

Bomn looks on with concern. Been looking at her that way for a while now. She flops her head forward and notices.

"What!" she demands, aggravated. "What do you want? Want me to say I let the case drop out from under me because I was too busy chasing Burgess? Fine! But what do I do now?"

"Go home," Bomn says like it's the most obvious solution in the world because it is. "Spend some time with Bob and Leigh. A pending son-in-law even?"

Em smirks ever so slightly. "I can't believe you're the one wearing the engagement ring..."

Bomn's left ring finger indeed has a ring on it.

"Stop saying that. It's my grandfather's fraternity ring. I've been wearing it since before you even met me."

"It's funny to say it," Em admits, though lethargically. She leans back in her chair again, smirks.

"I'm giving you a pass, since levity is good for you right now."

Em softens a little but is otherwise resolute. She holds up some of the *UPWU* documents. "When you're trying to shoot the sparrow outta the sky and the fatted goose waddles right on past your toes, you still gotta shoot the sparrow for lunch. It's all you have left."

"Just be sure the bird hasn't flown."

THE FILES ARE SPREAD AROUND even more haphazardly now. Em's still watching the video, still pawing through her files, and Bomn's *still* watching Em with concern.

The detective is sinking lower and lower in her seat. She puts her fingers to the pulse in her neck again. Bomn leans forward. He's seen this a thousand times with Em but he's really concerned now. He walks over to her chair and hunkers down beside her, hand on her shoulder.

She looks to him, appreciative, but she can't stop her face bunching up a little. Bunching up in some sort of pain. "The strike fund's intact," she says like it's the hardest thing to admit in the world because it is. "She's paying her workers. Been paying them this whole time without fail." She looks off at nothing now. Exhales. "Got me again." Look goes dire. "That was her plan all along. Send me running around in circles trying to hang her up, knowing I could only ever exonerate her. Played me like a fiddle while Rome burned."

Em's focus returns to her doting partner. She pats Bomn on his head affectionately. The patting gradually transforms into the use of his head as leverage to lift herself out of her seat. She starts collecting her files, dumping them into the garbage can whenever she feels she has as big an armful as she can manage. The Saint video plays on in the background.

She puts on a pretend brave face, takes out her phone and puts her earbud in. She waves the phone at Bomn. "Let's catch some new bad guys."

Bomn's unconvinced.

"*Come on partner,*" she implores. She starts checking voicemails. There's only one and it's from Hack.

"Hi Em," says Hack's voice through the earbud. "Thought I'd reach out. Sydney and Aylynn are hanging in there but they're having a hard time accepting what happened with Charles. Me too really. For what it's worth, I think that note's bullshit too. Charlie wasn't taking the company online exclusive. He asked me and the agents about business stuff all the time. About how we and our wives shopped. Most of us said *our purchasing preferences came down to price but if we needed the item right away, it's in store.* He said that's why Park's keeping the hybrid model."

...double-minimum-wage...

Em's attention diverts to the Saint video still playing.

"...The immediacy," Hack continues. "Now, how did he put it..."

But the video demands her focus.

She's reversing it to a point where Reime speaks. She hits play. Reime's saying,

Why don't you ask your soon-to-be former members that when these investments are paying them double-minimum-wage at Park...

"'Use one hundred percent of the in-store market to subsidize competing for one hundred percent of the online market'..."

Em reverses the video again, hits play.

Why don't you ask your soon-to-be former members that when these investments are paying them double-minimum-wage at Park...

"...Point is, he was as much invested in the physical as the online..."

Em's pensive as hell.

"I'm rambling," Hack concludes. "I know you're off the case, but I thought I'd reach out to you with this first. Talk to you later."

Why don't you ask your soon-to-be former members that when these investments are paying them double-minimum-wage at Park...

She stares up at the ceiling. *"Paying their wages... Competing for one hundred percent of the online market..."* She grabs her trashed files and starts digging through them again. Bomn's concerned all over again. Tesque sees this too and heads over.

"Thought you gave up the ghost, Gray."

Em's talking to herself at this point, reading through a particular page. "She's been paying them the whole time. For weeks and weeks."

"Yeah, I heard ya say that."

Em leaps out of her chair and grabs Tesque by the face. "No you beautiful bastard! The money's been paying the workers the whole time! It's all there! Never not! That was the point all along! She actually wants to see them through this strike paid in full."

She flies out of the office on a mission.

Chapter 14

Solidarity

Burgess is at one of her trailers' entrances, accompanied by her bodyguard Carl. A mass of picketers cheer in her direction as she opens the trailer door. There're so many more on the plaza this time around. She turns back to face the crowd, waves, and...

"Solidarity!"

Crowd erupts. She enters her trailer, Carl staying behind to guard the entrance.

BURGESS FUMBLES ALONG THE SIDE of the wall toward her office trying to find the light switch. *CLICK!* The light goes on but barely illuminates a path to her desk. She moves to it, sits, and starts reaching for her desk lamp when...

KNOCK! KNOCK! KNOCK!

"Come in," she says in haste, too busy trying to find that second switch.

A figure enters and stands in the dark of the trailer entrance.

Burgess is still groping around for the lamp. "What did I forget Carl?"

"I remember when you used to whup us up into a frenzy like that."

CLICK! Desk lamp goes on as Em walks into the light. Burgess is a split-second wary, then relieved, then annoyed.

"Can you get a restraining order against a cop?"

"Yes," Em says obligingly. "Look, I'm not here to fight with you."

"Then what do you want?"

Em sinks defeated-like into a chair opposite Burgess' side of the desk.

"I wanted to tell you, you win. I've chewed over every piece of gristle I could chew here, and your strike fund's clean. Money's going to the workers. *Robust. Eighty percent.* Everything as you stated." Em swallows hard. "I was wrong."

"Of course you were," Burgess assures. "But that's not why you're here. When's the other shoe going to drop? It always does with you. Is this where you tell me you're going to get me on the union's taxes? Coercion? Extortion? Racketeering? What?"

"No. Union's clean. Can't get ya on any of that. You know it."

"So why are you here?"

Em sits upright like she cares about her posture all a sudden.

"Union's clean. Union's clean and I can't help but think if I had just worked with you from the beginning instead of against you, things would be different. If we had only learned to work together, things would have been so much better. *Solidarity* Nina." Never been more upright. "If I had just worked with you instead of working against you..."

Now she slouches. She was going to say what she was going to say straight, but it must have taken a lot out of her.

With this concession, the detective's investigation of Burgess' union impropriety is officially over. For good.

Chapter 15

"If I had Just Worked with You from the Beginning, Things Would be Different..."

"That's the smartest thing I've heard you say yet," Burgess gloats. She's testing Em.

Em just sits there absorbing Burgess' victory, unmoved, not reacting at all.

Burgess comprehends. *The investigation really is over?* She cocks her head at Em now and, in a move uncharacteristic of her, softens. She actually looks sympathetic. "Listen," she says, still condescending a little because she can't help it—but also in earnest. "I—I'm not completely blameless here Em. If I hadn't provided you those files... I know that wild goose chase I sent you on caused the Park case—"

"I can't help but think," Em interrupts. "If I had just kept my mouth shut about your stealing our funds, you'd still be with the nurses. You never would have thrown in with the parcel workers and you never would have gotten to the point where you did what you did." Burgess' eyes narrow. Em goes on. "Things would be different and I wouldn't have to do what *I* have to do."

"And what, exactly, is that?" Burgess asks, patience peeling.

"Arrest you."

Executive affects a chuckle, real theatric. "For what?"

"The murder of Bertrand Park." Dead serious.

"Ha!"

"The murder of Charles Reime. The murder of Chester Pearson."

"I get it. Nurse *turned* cop *turned* stand-up comedian. You really will never change."

Em's still stone at this. "You're under arrest Nina."

Burgess tries for stoic herself. "Y—your Major told me personally that the private investigator who killed Park wrote a letter of confession."

"Interesting you brought that up," Em says, sitting back up. "You wrote it." Burgess scoffs again. Em could give a shit. "In Pearson's note—"

"Pearson?"

"*Touché*. The private investigator you hired to do your killing, Nina. Pearson said all incriminating evidence was destroyed *after* Park presented it to Reime. No way Park gave this evidence back to Pearson. It's what Park paid for after all. Pearson also speculated as to how Reime figured out about the investigation. Again, no way Pearson would speculate over something he'd demand Reime tell him up front. They were meeting in person... *according to the note...* and Pearson needed as much incriminating evidence on Reime as he could get... *again, according to the note*. He'd get it. Pearson had no reason to lie either since he was already setting Reime up for conspiracy and confessing to murder in the process."

"I can't keep track of all this nuance Gray. I've never seen the note."

"*Touché* again. The note's full of holes. A forgery. It was hastily written by somebody using Pearson and not a career criminal like Pearson himself. He knows too much about the ins and outs of killing and blackmail to commit such inconsistencies. Also, no one in his position would be stupid enough to incriminate himself like that. What if someone found the note before Pearson kicked it?"

"So what? What if this Pearson guy didn't write the note? We've just as much evidence you wrote it at this point as we do anyone else."

"The note's a forgery but not a complete fiction. Note says Park confronted a guilty party. I think he did and that guilty party was *you*. He confronted you and you paid Pearson to kill him. Then you paid Pearson to kill Reime. Pearson was on the lam so maybe you promised to get him out of the country or something similar? But you were hiding in the shadows that night and once Pearson shot Reime dead you filled Pearson full of holes and planted the murder weapon on Reime. Your two co-conspirators gone in one fell swoop. That's all your loose ends tied."

"Two co-conspirators? I'm trying to follow your fiction here... So far, I've only *conspired* with Pearson. What did I conspire with Reime?"

"What Park confronted you over: Reime artificially inflating your strike fund." Burgess' ice melts a little. Em notices. "Reime was shorting your stock knowing the strike would drive your prices down and buying up Park-Mart knowing the strike would drive those prices up. He then poured that money back into your fund.

"Now, your taking donations from Reime isn't illegal *per se*. He's a private citizen and he exercised no control over union affairs. What Reime did wasn't illegal *per se*, either. He wanted your union to do what unions do and nothing more. But, what he did was certainly unethical." Em takes a breath, looks a little melancholy. "Bertrand Park was a nice man. His workers had a saying about him. Said he never gave people the benefit of the doubt. Never gave it because there was never ever the thought of any ill at hand to invalidate. The man perished the thought. Charlie broke his heart..." Another breath. "Some call this aspect of Bertie's character naive. I call it refreshing.

"It's why he thought you were a nice person too. He approached you before Reime, therefore, hoping you'd do the right thing and help him put an end to the donations. You and he could deal with Reime without involving the board and your union. What Bertie didn't know was that you were in on Reime's scheme all along. Of course, he *would* have known, had he known, that your and Reime's collusion certainly made all this a crime... If only in a poetic sense."

Burgess shakes her head in incredulity. "You understand that the veracity of all this hinges on Charles Reime, of all people, making hundreds of millions in investments only to give it all away subsidizing a labor strike? If it weren't for the tragic circumstances—for Bertie—I would almost find this entertaining."

"Don't think for a second I fail to appreciate the fine line a person in your position must walk, Nina..."

"How's that?"

"Having to appear stalwart, even arrogantly defiant in the face of these accusations while still feeling for your victim. Too much scoffing and too little grief and you seem callous, apathetic, guilty. Too much emotion and too little protest and you seem almost repentant, indifferent to the accusations, guilty. A delicate balance. But don't hurt yourself. You're not in front of a jury. Not yet."

"Won't get to that. Your story's not even a fiction Gray but farce. Preposterous. Though I must admit, I am curious as to what, on your tale, explains my jeopardizing my workers—not to mention Reime's deathbed conversion."

"Crude."

"Just a turn of phrase."

"*Politics. Economics,*" Em recommences. "Show management that you can subsidize the strike indefinitely and they'll cave to virtually any demand you make. Unionized workers are happy to stay on strike with what you're paying them and, for your successes, any potential scab wants in on the union not the warehouse. Alom and EchoNet need workers but the workers don't need them. They'll cave and you'll be a legend among union leaders what with the exorbitant pay increases, record entry wages, benefits, and all the rest you've guaranteed. That's your angle. It's always political for you."

"And where's the economics?"

"Reime's pouring money into your strike fund prolonged the strike. This drove your share prices further down and his share prices further up, providing him with even more investment earnings to pump back into the fund. Say Alom and EchoNet had refused to cave, then Reime's investing would have cycled on until both companies were bled dry and failed completely. Say they had caved, then they'd never have been able to afford your demands. There'd be layoffs sending workers to Park-Mart and an increase in Alom and EchoNet prices sending shoppers there too. Park grows, Alom and Echo shrink. This means more layoffs for the latter two companies meaning more business and labor for the former. Park grows even larger and the cycle continues until Alom and Echo fail completely. Cave or not, it's failure. Failure that would have benefitted you and Reime all the way down. Park-Mart corners the market on physical and online shopping and you're the next John L. Lewis. Trillions for millions. Until Bertie threw a monkey into that wrench, of course."

Burgess looks a little relieved. *Looks.* "Congratulations. You've saved your fantasy from complete farce. But it's still a fantasy. The magnum opus of a woman with a badge and an unhealthy obsession."

"I had help writing it."

"There's someone out there as deluded as you?"

"Reime." Em takes out her phone. "He all but laid out the blueprint for your scheme the night you debated." Em hits play on her phone. It's Reime saying, *Tell that to your soon-to-be former members...*

"He said that and I *all but* accused him of insider trading. If the SEC wasn't investigating him already, they would be after that night."

"To clarify, you accused him of immorality. In fact, you all but agreed that his investments were above board. Clever misdirection." Em puts the phone down. "But you're right, the SEC has been investigating him. They hit a brick wall. They were trying to get him on insider trading. They care where the money's *coming from* not where it's *going*. They were looking for an industry insider helping Reime when Reime was the insider all along."

"Alright, we've got an explanation for Park's murder. It's consistent detective. It's not fact—"

"You sound like my boss..."

"It's just a story of yours, Gray. That's all it's ever been."

"Until the facts come pouring in. The circumstances of Reime's murder necessitate a formal investigation into his financial and business relationships. It's already underway and Park-Mart board members and the SEC are playing ball. And that's where we get you."

"You'll never tie me to any such scheme."

"Already have." Em tosses some SEC documents onto Burgess' desk.

Burgess recognizes the SEC emblem. "SEC records? From an SEC you say has nothing on Reime?"

"It's not what they *have* that makes you suspect. It's what they *don't*. The list of all formal complaints filed in regard to Reime's recent investments is massive. Every dog and their body has filed a TCR against Reime for insider trading." Em pauses a second. "Except you."

"We concern ourselves with the labor market, not the stock market, detective."

Em throws more documents onto the desk. "Except you don't. According to the records you so graciously provided, you've personally filed dozens of formal complaints against investors shorting your stocks, only never against Reime." Em gestures to the files like she's saying *go ahead, see for yourself.* "Answer me this Nina, what do you think would happen if we got our hands on a list of major investors shorting Alom and Echo and indexed all who you *didn't* file a TCR against? Obviously Reime's not subsidizing your strike single-handedly. If you are colluding to inflate the fund, someone on that list is bound to sell you out for a better deal."

Burgess slumps a little. "Go ahead and look, you won't tie me to Reime."

"Already have."

No irony from Burgess anymore, just an *oh come on!* face. "How?"

"*One-hundred and twelve-thousand three-hundred and seventy-eight dollars and twenty-four cents.*"

Burgess gestures a *what's that supposed to mean* Gesture. Em tosses more files.

"Reime's a donor."

"Donor deposits are redacted."

"Not withdrawals. Scan down about a third of the way on page four." Em flicks her fingers along the pages, phantom flipping in an attempt to motivate Burgess to read faster.

What Burgess sees is,

*HASH DEPOSIT-84726: $112,378.24 (********) Balance $18,921,712,845.27 ***CANCELLED****

HASH WITHDRAWAL-84727: $112,378.24 (ASC 24601) Balance $18,921,600,467.03

"Now, halfway down the next page."

HASH DEPOSIT-84882: $112,378.24 (********) Balance $18,921,712,845.27

"Needle in a haystack," Em insists. "But it looks like someone made a deposit, canceled it, and the money was automatically returned. Later it was redeposited. The withdrawal account is Reime's charity organization."

"So Reime gave us some cash and you found him thanks to a glitch. He's one of thousands and thousands."

"Except it wasn't a glitch. Reime cancelled the deposit *in-transfer*. Cold feet maybe? Could be he was still figuring out his foundation's banking system?"

"What do you mean *Cold feet*?"

"Reime would never make deposits using an account that could be traced to him. Not unless... Mutually assured destruction. You send cash to him from this account, he back to you from his. One time. He blows the whistle or tries to blackmail you, you got the goods on him. You blow the whistle or try to blackmail him, *vice versa*. The second deposit was the one that took and that's why you didn't notice the canceled attempt on the previous page. I'm sure we'll find a similar deposit from you to Reime among his financial records. See this?" Em holds her phone up to Burgess again. The screen displays Reime's note with the sum of money and coordinates on it,

112378247?

41 43'57'NICE 49 56'49'WORK

"That number was important enough to Reime to get him to evade protective custody and drive to the coordinates pictured. It's an impossible coincidence that this seemingly random number turned out to represent the exact sum of money Reime donated to your strike fund. If you're paying attention Nina, this sum doesn't just link you to Reime, it links you to Reime's murder."

Burgess pushes herself backward a few inches away from her desk. She leans just her torso forward in a ridiculous hunch. Taps her fingers on the edge of the walnut like she's typing out what she's about to say. "*Facts*," she almost sings. "*Best when they're cold and complete and conspiring, composed... Conspiring to put man's lusts in repose.*" She leans back into her chair. "I think I'd like to call my lawyer."

"Poetry notwithstanding... Because it doesn't... That's a good idea. You'll be expected to account for how a person as vocal as you in your condemnation of Reime's investment practices wouldn't include him in a list of dozens of SEC complaints. More importantly, you'll need to account for how a random number used to compel Reime to leave police custody... for a location that would ultimately be the site of his murder... is the same as the sum of money he donated to you." Em gives Burgess a second to process this. "We have more than enough to arrest you on suspicion to conspire murder. Better get a good lawyer too because whether or not you get off, if the public catches wind of your involvement with Reime, your political career will be over."

Burgess gets pensive for just a second, but a wide-eyed, shudder-filled second. She sighs, opens her left-hand drawer. Em notices.

"I know how ya feel..."

Burgess pulls a small handgun out of the drawer and lays it on the desk, her left hand holding it as it lies.

"...Yer feelin' like murder. You've killed already in cold blood and paid someone else to kill you another. Maybe two. Why not do it again if it'll cover your tracks? Well, I'm not going to give you a *you're only making it worse for yourself* kinda appeal because you're not making it worse for yourself. You're gonna fry for what you've done already. I'm not going to tell you you'll never get away with it because you will. I'm your last obsessive, harassing, stalking loose end. I'm not going to tell you not to do it because *redemption starts now*. There's not a shred of conscience left in you. I'm only going to tell you this: I'm a faster draw than you underwater, so if you try what yer thinkin' yer gonna die the rat that stole my sisters' livelihoods."

Burgess looks anodyne for a second then... She lifts the gun and stands to shoot! Her target's lightning quicker though. Em bolts out of her seat and...

BANG! BANG! BANG! BANG! BANG!

Five dead-eyed in the elbow joint of Burgess' unfired-gun-holding arm, and...

BANG! BANG! BANG! s'more until that arm rips completely off!

SPLOOSH-SPLATCH!

(Gun obviously falls from Burgess' grip as the arm tears away).

There's another little bitty tear rolling out the corner of Em's eye. Then...

She rushes over to Burgess, whipping off her belt as she goes. She ties the belt as a tourniquet around Burgess' bleeding stump.

"Thought you said you'd kill me," Burgess groans, weary and faint.

"I said you'd *die* and you will. You'll die one day and you'll still die that rat. Only now you'll die a rat in complete and utter disgrace."

"Could still get off ya know... Could say the *obsessive, harassing, stalking,* maniac attacked me."

Em ignores this. Puts the end of her belt in Burgess' only hand available and gestures for her to keep it cinched tight.

"Now, I'm not gonna cuff ya because quite frankly I'm not sure of the logistics of that at this point, but you're not gonna let go of that belt anyway if you don't want to bleed to death..." She wrenches Burgess' stump skyward. "Arm up."

EM AND BURGESS EXIT THE trailer, Em holding Burgess by the collar. Carl and the picketers stand just outside the door looking intimidating, like maybe they're not going to let Em take their savior away. Then...

The crowd parts like some sort of sea. Em walks Burgess through the opening as, one by one, the picketers start removing their *UPWU* pins, throwing them at their president's feet. As Em keeps on walking her suspect, we notice something peculiar in her right breast pocket. A closer look reveals the top of a pair of glasses barely peeking out at us. Em keeps walking, passing someone familiar amidst the crowd continuing to renounce their *UPWU* ties. Gregory waves his phone. It displays a pocket-camera image broadcasting from Em's coat. He nods. Em nods back. She moves out of the crowd and the parting closes up behind her.

A picketer leans down to a dropped picket sign. He takes out a pastel crayon from his pocket, picks up the sign and crosses out the *UPWU* logo at the top. He hands his crayon to the picketer beside him and picketer starts crossing out her *UPWU* logo too. We pull out over the strikers moving back to the line, *UPWU-less* signs waving.

We're back on Em now, leading Burgess away from the crowd slowly receding behind her. Burgess looks silent and defeated. Em looks tired.

They get to the car. Em shuts Burgess into the passenger side seat and moves around to the driver's side. On her way, she puts her two fingers to her neck for the millionth time. She stops at the driver's side door, fingers still on her pulse.

...BUMPUMP BUMPUMP BUMPUMP BUMPUMP BUMPUMP BUMPUMP...

It's unremitting, faultless. Em smiles the deepest smile of relief. She gets into the car and peels away.